THE WICKLOW WAY

And other Irishman's Tales

DOUG MCPHILLIPS

ALSO BY DOUG MCPHILLIPS

OTHER VISIONARY STORIES

POETRY

FROM DARKNESS TO LIGHT

AWAKE TO MY GUTTED DREAMS

NOVELS

THE SWORD OF DISCERNMENT

SANTIAGO TRAVELLER

I, PROPHET

WE IS ME UPSIDE

MASTERS AT MY TABLE

THE GURU OF JERUSALEM

DOUG MCPHILLIPS 2021

ISBN 978-0-64-5245-9-6

NATIONAL; LIBRARY OF AUSTRALIA CATALOGUE-IN- PUBLICA-TION DATA: AUTOBIOGRAPHY-WALKING THE CAMINO, ALCOHOLICS ANONYMOUS. AUTHORS REFERENCES ARE THROUGHOUT THIS BOOK. IT IS A WORK OF FICTION. ALL CHAR-ACTERS IN THIS NOVEL WHO ONCE LIVED ARE NOW AN ACT OF FICTION. ANY RESEMBLANCE TO ACTUAL EVENTS OR PERSONS, LIVING OR DEAD, IS ENTIRELY COINCIDENTAL.

Introduction:

I had been caught up in the material world and had closed down my heart for a long time to the spiritual. To get it back it came in a calamity with much sorrow and pain. There seemed to be no way out and I had collapsed into a deep depression. The answer came in a cry for help. It came on a mountain path, it came in the villages en route alone and with others as I walked the way of St. James in a new acceptance of letting go to the God of my own understanding. My vision this time was to go all the way to Finisterre. Tramp the way to the north western point of the mainland. A place known in medieval times as " the end of the earth." I was not to know at that time that I would then be guided to Dublin, Ireland. Whisked away to the isle of my ancestors, to tramp the mountains of the Wicklow Way, tramp the Aran Island coastline of the east and ride a push-bike down the west coast. Before this journey was complete I would walk near 1200 kilometres; before the insanity came to cease completely in my mental, physical and spiritual exhaustion.

I had been letting go of all that I once thought I was about and in the end the spiritual was not as expected. It came in the form of more creativity outpouring, a continual litany of poetry, stories and songs. It would take me sometime to release from my defects of character, to accept who I am, to hand over to a Power greater than self whom I chose to call God before I got it. The play of inner secret and not the world at large, not the hand in the dark nor the need for sexual gratification, explained through my awakening through myth to love. It is still taking a great deal of nothingness to reach the void. To be and not just to do.

CONTENT:

For Mirjana

CHAPTER 1.

TO BEGIN AGAIN ON A NEW WAY

My thoughts drifted again. I was crossing the great Meseta in my mind. it was autumn; raining, windy and cold. Thankful for a warm under garment, a hooded rain jacket and an umbrella, I had come prepared this time. Recalling my looking at the rain clouds above and the lush landscape for as far as the eye could see, it had seemed like I was in the Garden of Eden. Crops of wheat and barley, grapes and berries grew by the roadside as I passed and it was like spring rain had returned and the farmers had taken advantage of this freak weather. I found out later, it had been raining consistently through the summer and into this early autumn. The farmers had already harvest - ed their crops but were having another crack at it with approving weather, before winter set in. On my first journey on the Masada, it had been a forty two degree heat for most of the summer days of that 2013 tramp and it was altogether different. It was dry and dusty, like one would expect of a desert. I had crossed the one hundred kilometre flat plain with very little water, and far too much weight in my back pack. Not many pilgrims dared to cross that high plateau of Spain in the summer months, but I had been mainly alone with my boring thoughts as I crossed and my repetitive steps and bleakness of mind kept me on track. It was not the landscape that had lifted my spirit, nor the monotonous repetitive tramping. It was the sky rich with colours and diverse clouds.

The Masada may well have been a long haul back then and a trudge of endurance, but the endless horizons and wide open spaces made it all worthwhile. The cities that had broken the monotony were vibrant and held a beauty and awe beyond compare, and the influence of " The rain in Spain flows mainly on the plain." I had been drenched to the bone all day, and every day on that crossing and had a dreadful chest infection and rasping cough to boot. I had been thankful for my stays in the fair cities of Burgos and Leon to recover from my health issues before returning to the road again. It was the life I led then, one day up and the next down, like the track itself, never knowing what or whom I would encounter on my weary way, but always mindful of new horizons, shackled to my back pack of necessary possessions and my ever onward trudging. Three Camino's had inspired me to write of my adventures, fired my imagination with stories and songs that seemed to come from the ether. The Masada had inspired such notable characters as Don Quixote de la Mancha, the spiritual and mystical St.Teresa of Avila and St. John of the Cross. It was a wilderness experience for me with so many fictitious characters that had appeared to me on the plain and so many real ones, like Mohammad and St.James and St. Anthony. So it was no small wonder that I would return to the land of my inspirations.

My mind began to drift now to Jesus and his forty days and nights in the desert. The lenient time was over and He had fasted and lived, like John the Baptist on wild berries and perhaps magic mushrooms! At least in John's case it seemed more likely when one delves into the prophecies of the Book of Revelations. I did a mental reckoning as I tramped The Way and concluded that there is no man, discounting those of saintly disposition, who dared to dream and scheme for personal gratification, prestige and reward. These men of great standing allow themselves to disregard the high ground of morality in favour of their dark deed of personal gain which, when actioned upon could be justified to their own benefit and that of others. In a sometimes not so small way I had built my own family tree working for such enterprises and ultimately myself, to raise a family, provide for the education of my children with an ultimate goal of fulfilling my personal dreams and aspirations of financial independence. Working and borrowing from those very same bankers of the hand in the dark in the process to fulfil my personal desire. I was no different, I needed money to survive, a place to live, and personal goals to achieve, but in the afternoon of my life, what was more important, my past mindsets or my future freedom? Living in the now in a peaceful state is fine for a while but the old itch that just had to be scratched still persisted.

I had made my way in the world and enjoyed my progress. Though not all perfect I was sustained by a worthwhile career, enjoying the fruits of my labour with good food, fashionable clothing, the best of shelter and initially a happy marriage. I had financed and provided a good education for my kids, and later a costly divorce was fought for the sharing of earthly spoils. I had a conditioned belief in God, the Church and it was by my own choice and effort that life went the way it did, good, bad or indifferent. But who helped me along the way to get where I had got too? Yes, I had to admit that I brought the conditioning of the hand in the dark consciousness over my own inner spirit. I had chosen a career to work as one of their many pawns in the game, borrowed money from the banks to get were I got to corporately and later in my own business enterprises. Here in this life and without their system, would I have had the ability to do that and would I now be able to survive in body, mind and spirit without being a part of their system? I had to admit as I walked along, it is all very well to cast a critical eye over history but what would my life have been if I had not adhered to the dark hand rules and followed my own consciousness of good intent? What would have happened if I always listened and lived by the Golden Rule and not using my egocentric nature to work, taking chances and blinding out my conscious goodness? The choice is always ours, to follow the Golden Rule of the heart by living to love Godlike principles for our betterment or continue to be possessed by our basic instincts which ultimately lead us to destruction and death. In my own case it was almost mandatory to my survival and that of my family to overrule all the natural good of my heart with the use of my defects of character to get on in this world. In the end it came to nothing for me.

I had walked The Way of the Templar Knights and was once more reminiscing my past walk in search of the history of the Portuguese ship that had wrecked on the south east coast of Victoria, during the Spice Wars in the Age of Discovery. The Caravel is known in Australia as "the Mahogany Ship" had motivated me to walk The Way again and prompted the writing of another book-"The Santiago traveler- My Pilgrimage to a hidden treasure." During my research for the book I had discovered the blue print for the Caravel cargo ships and its story from drawings held in the bowels of the Church of St. John the Baptist in Tomar, Portugal. Thinking of Henry 'The Navigator" who commanded the Templar fleet for Portugal and the amazing ability of the Knights Templar, the earliest of The Free-Masons, I considered not only their leadership qualities, their skills as horseman, military genius, protectors of the poor, but also of their ability as the earliest of money traders and indeed bankers. Columbus on his voyage of discovery of America was backed and financed by these same Knights Templar who went on to become the Free-Masons. Like Mayer Amschel of the Rothschild and his creation of a banking dynasty. He raised a red flag meaning 'Rothchild' in German translation. It being symbolically embossed with a red cross upon a white background which had a dual meaning; the blood of Christ on the Cross for the God of the Light and the blood cross and white semen of satanic ritual. Near a century before Columbus the Templars had a similar standard. Before Columbus set foot on American soil the Templars were already trading in the Americas with natives there. The earliest of that land's history as well as the Templars own their tale of ethnic cleansing, imposition of power, slavery, mass exploitation and the worship of wealth. The Rothschilds like many other banking dynasties followed the principles of lending and learnt it from the secret of the templar Knights.

It had not been a good night's sleep in that Albergue a Escuela, where I shared a room with two young female pilgrims who were sleeping soundly in the double bunks opposite me. I had sat on the verandah until the clock struck one, listening to their steady breathing through the open doorway behind me. Sitting there reflecting on Christ's final hours before his crucifixion until the chill of the night air drove me under the cover of my sleeping bag and into the land of nod for a few hours. I was up before dawn, weary but ready for another day's journey on The Way. The little township of Laguna de Castilla, the last two clicks on the Camino in Castilla had a colourful cement marker about 1km out of town with the sword of The Templars at its head, the sign of the pilgrim shell on the left of its base and on its right the circular

stars emblem of the EU. Between these two symbolic stellar the official mark noted 'entrance into Galicia,' the final region on the Camino
where Santiago de Compostela is located. I stood for a long time at
the marker considering my journey thus far and the reason for this pilgrimage. Most of the world's major religions have a tradition of pilgrimage. The Haji, a pilgrimage to Mecca is a specific symbolic action
and one of the five pillars of Islam. The Jewish faith pilgrimages centre
around Jerusalem and the sight of the former Jewish temple. Buddhist
pilgrims flock to important places from the life of Buddha and the Ba-
ha'i pilgrims walk the steps of their temple to Haifa, Israel. The Bible,
even from its beginning in Hebrew scripture, speaks of a people on
the move, wandering through the desert being led by and provided for
by God. Some say the Maji who traveled from the east to visit the
baby Jesus were the first Christian pilgrims. Others in Christ's adult-
hood had made journeys for healing or to hear him teach. At least that
is what the New Testament would have us believe and I with my baptism and upbringing belong to the latter Catholic faith and even today
continue in my struggle to believe.   In my disbelief I made my way
past the marker on the entrance to Galicia along this Camino once
again, a pilgrimage to find some reason for living and hoping, on this
Good Friday morn, as I entered the final leg towards my goal at the
Compostela de Santiago. It was as I journeyed that the sky turned
from the moon shadows of the night to the first rays of sunlight pierc-
ing my troubled mind. The morning sun had risen like the first morning
and the birds were already singing as I made my way through the
cobblestone streets of Santiago. I breathed a sigh of relief as I entered
the square overshadowed by the immensity of the Cathedral that
stood before me. Already the workers were on the scaffolding of the
steeples applying the final touches of their trade to the stonework on
the phallic like twin towers steeples. It seemed almost renewed in the
renovation process.

I had visited this Cathedral thrice before, attended the Mass for the
Pilgrims, visited the shrine and bones of St. James, the Apostle of
Christ, the first of Christ Apostles to suffer martyrdom at the hands of
Herod the King, traditionally known as Herod Agrilla. James the
stronger who was known as 'Son of Thunder' because of his temper,
was the first of the Apostles to die for his faith. He was beheaded in 44
A.D. in Jerusalem, the Holy City of the Jewish faithful and his bodily
remains reported floated on a stone barge Viking style, towards the
coast of Spain. It was there he was buried and promptly forgotten
about for over 700 years, or so the story tellers would have us believe.
James' bones were reportedly rediscovered and symbolically used to
bolster up Christian faith in the war against the Muslims in 813-14 A.D.
They were transported and buried in a crypt under the altar here at the
Cathedral, or so the story goes. The Saint that now lay in the crypt in
front of me as I knelt to say a prayer still not believing that it was his
bones within the Ark like Temple that lay before me .I said a prayer-

none-the-less just in case, in my superstition, I was somehow proven to be wrong. It had been a long hard slog into Santiago that morning and not for the first time, I climbed the stairs of 'the Quintana of the Dead' where the first of the local traders were opening their shop shutters for the coming throng of Pilgrim tourists. Those Pilgrims who would venture forth in their search for a gift of remembrance of their pilgrimage for themselves or a loved one back home. I made my way up the next level of stairs on to 'the Quintana of the Living' and entered the first of many cafes and taverns at this level. The waitress of the buxom kind, a middle aged Spanish women, whose face was far too weathered and old for her apparent years, offered me a kindly smile and a room high above in the attic. The room had been freshly painted and the white lime paint stung my eyes and my nostrils as I entered. There was no water, or shower, but it had a narrow bed and that's all that really mattered to a weary traveler. A small bathroom shared with adjoining room tenants, a toilet and a hot shower was a gift at that moment in time. So after completing each bodily task, I dressed in fresh clothing from my small backpack. What was in that pack was all my worldly possessions on my Pilgrimage, but it was enough and I had adequate monies to see my way through another week before returning home to Australia.

Looking back at the attic room far above the cobblestone street of Santiago and the city, my mind returned once more to the small room that the Apostles met in just after their Saviour's Crucifixion. After Mary's words to her friends and Christ followers, Peter had remarked: "Sister, we know that the Saviour loved you more than other women (John 11:5, Luke 10:38-42) tell us the words of the Saviour which you have in mind since you know them; and we do not, nor have we heard them." Mary answered and said, *"What is hidden from you I will impart to you." She began: "I saw the Lord in a vision and I said to him "Lord, I saw you today in a vision, and he answered and said to me," Blessed are you, since you did not waiver at the sight of me. For where the mind is, there is your countenance." (Matt 6:21). I said to him, "Lord, the mind which sees the vision, does not see it through the soul or through the spirit?'" The Saviour answered and said, "It sees it neither through the soul nor through the spirit, but the mind, which is between the two, which sees the vision, and it is..."*

"...and Desire said, 'I did not see you descend; but now I see you rising. Why do you speak falsely, when you belong to me?' The soul answered and said,' I saw you, but you did not recognize me; I serve you as a garment and you did not recognize me.' After it had said this, it went joyfully and gladly away. Again it came to the third power, Ignorance, This power questioned the soul: "Whither are you going? You were bound in wickedness, you were bound indeed. Judge not" (Matt 7:1) and the soul said, 'Why do you judge me, when I judged not? I was bound, though I did not bind. I was not recognized, but I recognized that all will go free, things both earthly and heavenly. After the

soul had left the third power behind, it rose upward, and saw the fourth power, which had seven forms. The first form is darkness, the second is desire, the third ignorance, the fourth the arousing of death, the fifty the kingdom of the flesh, the sixth, the wisdom of the folly of the flesh, the seventh is wrathful wisdom. "

It was mid-morning when I made my way past the Cathedral to visit the many gifts shops and eateries that adorned the streets of Santiago. Visiting the fish markets, I selected the best of the days catch and made my way to a nearby fish shop watching the proprietor cooking and preparing my meal for my immediate consumption. Taking a bench nearby, I enjoyed the local cuisine of boiled peppered octopus followed by a generous serve of fish, chips and salad washed down with 'sin 00' non- alcoholic beer. Refreshed and with a full belly I wandered the cobblestone streets to the idyllic Alameda Park where locals met to relax and chat away the day, in the shade of an old palm and olive trees. As I had done on previous visits to the park, I made my way to the stone bench "banco ac'ustico," the bench of whispers. Designed in a semi- circle, one could place one's head up against the back of the seat and hear the conversation of the voice that tracked and became louder as it was received by the listener all the way across to the other end. Careful not to speak but observe the comings and goings I noted that even today lovers seated apart were speaking quietly to one another on that bench. The tradition of the sometimes called 'lovers bench' had firmly became a well- known destination for innocent trysts during the Franco years, when an emphasis on strict social morals prevented touch or talking in public. A suggested innocent walk in the park, where the betrothed just happen to be, often ended up in a secret romantic conversation on this Bench of whispers.

The lovers had moved on as had been the case on my previous visits and I found the stone bench an ideal place for my contemplation. I was considering my previous journeys, how far I had come since my first Camino in 2013, the outcomes that followed the later one in 2015 and again in 2017. I thought once again of Mary Magdalene's Gospel and her utterances in that little room of Christ's apostles after his death on the cross. Christ's words in her gospel, of the condition of being in the void of the mind and neither in body nor soul had me deep in thought. What had been my purpose in doing those three Camino's and indeed what had been gained or lost as a result? The seven participant in wrath at Mary encountered in her vision with Christ could certainly be applied to my pilgrimages, so I believed. The first of my journeys was the desire to let go of past pain and suffering as a result of the many tragic circumstances of my life over the previous decade. It had worked and I did let go a lot and fell into the dragon's mouth that had turned into a lotus flower off creative ideas. Flowing outcomes of this long journey came toward the centre of my being.

Yes. I had experienced the depths of despair and desire came to me as a participant of wrath, resulting in the planting of a seed of creative ideas which to some degree had grown into a bed of flowers in book and song. So desire had left me for a time and went blissfully away but returned on my next Camino in the form of a lover. At least I had ignorantly convinced myself that it was love which was like the nectar of fresh sweet wine but it quickly withered on the vine and dried up into a the pain of lust. It was not the first time I had fallen for this trap. "The power of the pussy." I mused to myself but like all 20:20 hindsight, nothing became of it. So I had bound myself in the wickedness of my nature like a lion seeing in dark places for a prey to devour. And here I was in judgement of myself and had fallen further into depression, through the power of darkness. The first of two participants in my wrath; desire and ignorance had embrace the third and death seemed for a while to be the only way out. The kingdom of the flesh had entangled me as a kind of soothing balm for my ailments but wisdom of my folly eventually prevailed and I had received counselling for my bitter anger of my lot in life. All these participants in my life journey I had let go of and another two books and another album was my means of expressing that which I now felt may be of some use to others on their life pilgrimage. I had tapped into something and it was not all about Doug. So silence had become my friend for a time, as I left that bench behind, perhaps for the last time and made my blissful way back on this journey of my soul. It was not for the things of this world that I now sought even though I had discovered much to benefit me in that regard, it was to live in this world but not of it that I now believed I had to attempt to find the balance.

A year had passed since that last Camino and I had returned feeling the effect of a hard journey on an old body, but I felt more content now than I had done for many a day. I was resigned to my retirement days of writing books and recording songs for those peoples both in the flesh and on social media who were interested in them. I had set out to do presentations on the subject matter of my pilgrimage entitled "What is a Pilgrimage and why do it?" and I was gaining some traction there too. However, the nagging thought of spending too much of my hard earned money in my dotage was quickly happening and I wondered how to revive the maxim "First to accumulate and then to conserve." There was the high moral ground of thought of what the Camino and the pursuit of a spiritual journey held for me until the day of my demise and an equally conflicting one of living in this world but not of it seeming somewhat impossible. The church was packed this Easter Sunday morning as I sat there with my new friend and partner and her many friends and associates for the reenactment of Christs last supper with the blessing of a giving of the host for the congregation and a homely by the priest on rising from the dead, ascension to that higher heavenly plain and how we are to play our part as living channels of the Holy spirit which is left for us to engage with in our handing over to The God of this Universal Church. At this point in time

I found it near impossible to embrace the mythology and symbolism of what I once believed in and carried it through, word and deed into the world that I now lived. Whilst I still made the effort to go to church on Christmas Day to celebrate the anniversary of Christ's birth and at Easter, to celebrate his rising from the dead on the third day and his ascension in the heavens, I found it difficult to accept the doctrines of faith and morals of this Universal religion. In particular, the double standards of the nuns and priests of religious orders, who had historically enforced their so called Christian moral discipline on us innocent children of by-gone days. It was no use complaining to a parent; as there was equally a warped view of spirituality. Words like "touch not your hands against the Lords anointed and remain guilty "still rang in my subconscious mind. "Do no evil say no evil "was the order of the day. Bare knuckle hits across the head were the order of the day for even a minor misdemeanour back then. The recall of us little boys in our shorts and school blues sitting on a bench outside in the cold of autumn morning with the fear of being hit, as our priestly one eyed alcoholic teacher swung a cracking stock whip over our heads in a desperate attempt to teach us Latin. The crack of it still rings in my head.   Yes, the memories of one's own pain were to a great degree lost in translation but not the memory of seeing fellow class mates being thrashed like slaves into a shaking bloody mess, scarred forever, so it now seems. I, like my many school mates, could forgive our religious teacher for their ill will and brutality for it was atypical of the times. But what I, like so many others of my class find hard to forgive and which still makes me angry   are the boys who suffered sexual abuse from these so called religious. Boys now men who still suffer the mental torment of being raped by so called men of God.

Religion, in my latter years has not answered much for me but I do miss the rituals and symbolism of the 'Faith of our Fathers Holy Faith.' I somehow lost my way with the religion of my youth when the world took precedence over religion. In the reality of the now the Priest followed the normal process of the offering of bread and wine representing the body and blood of Christ at his last supper. He turns to give his congregation his Easter homily. To his right stood the Pascal candle, the large white waxed-candle of white light which had been lit at the beginning of lent; the forty days of fasting symbolism; a reenactment of Christ retreat to the desert too fast and pray. It had now been extinguished of light, recognizing that lent was over and Christ risen. As the priest explains the cross is the central symbol which most clearly identifies it as a Pascal candle. The current day symbol of alpha and omega appear at the top and bottom of the cross signifying the beginning and the end, as specified in the Book of Revelation. Across the candle the current Easter year is shown and whilst the candle is lit every year for the Easter season, it really is not used throughout the year except for perhaps special occasions, like baptism and funerals. The candle means Passover, and relates to the Passover mystery of salvation. It is sometimes called the "Christ candle."

CHAPTER 2.

IN THE SHOES OF THE FISHERMAN

The Way was pleasant in the final isolated stage of my pilgrimage, walking through forest and villages, with the sea often in the sight to my goal of Muxia. The picturesque fishing town on the peninsula known as "The end of the earth" was a yesterday reality and a today dream of past faithful observance. Like the legend of Mary's apparition there in a stone ship delivering a message to a discouraged soldier of Christ, the apostle James. She had informed him, that despite his sense of failure in his mission to preach the word of God to a rabble of cult like inhabitants along the Iberian Peninsula, he had actually succeeded and should return to Jerusalem, his mission in Spain complete. He had built on her instruction and in her honour a rustic church overlooking the rocky shore and crashing waves. He had christened it 'Nosa Señora da Barca- Our Lady of the Boat' and the name still remained. Thousands had come over the centuries from far and wide to visit the image of Mary within the walls of the little church, dance in the streets of the village and eat the traditional 'caldareta' -fish stew, then carry the statue from the church   parading the virgin mother through the streets of Muxia.

I climbed the hill to the zero marker at the end of my Santiago de Compostela journey of The Way. One last glance overlooking the vast coastline that interrupted the wild Atlantic Ocean as its waves crashed repeatedly to the shore, I made my way back down the hill to the fishing village of Finisterre. It was to be the last day in my days of rest and renewal there, attempting my recovery from a strange illness that had overtaken me on my final leg of this journey. It was late afternoon as I sat by the water's edge sipping on a cool 'Sin 000' non- alcoholic beer and eating a small plate of octopus for entree, a traditional dish boiled and peppered to a taste delight. This I followed with a generous helping of local fish and potato chips. My stomach content, I turned to the fisherman preparing their nets in the hope of a good catch that evening at sea. Apparently the sardines were on the run and a good catch some ten kilometres out to sea was assured. The fisherman of the village always seem so certain of prosperity in this regard whenever you discussed fish with them. I gathered this had always been the case with centuries of fishing these Atlantic ocean waters. Perhaps it was the influence of their faith in the virgin mother who had appeared on this west coastline in a stone boat some 2000 years before that gave them such confidence of an assured catch.

Pedro the fisherman had gestured that I climb aboard his boat, as he and his fellow apostles of the sea stacked their nets in position to cast easily from the stern of the boat. The scent of fish and the sea stung my nostrils as I boarded. We ventured into deep water and the nets would soon be lowered some ten kilometre from shore in a favoured location of what the busy crew called 'the sardine run.' I had offered money to join them on their sea going quest ,Pedro on behalf of his apostles had politely refused.

The sea was not rough but the ebb and flow of the ocean felt like riding a rollercoaster. The little boat bobbed up and down like a cork and it seemed to me that the fisherman must have had magnetic boots as they seemed to grip the deck like glue, despite constant waves washing over them. They chatted and laughed a lot, whilst Pedro smoking his pipe steered the boat one handed, continually driving the bow directing into the swell. Occasionally the wave broke before the boat made it over the crest and Pedro, undeterred, just stayed the course. I had no fear in the hands of a master sailor and it was obvious to me that his fellow fisherman felt the same way. A daily trip at dusk like this; they must have experienced all kinds of conditions, from smooth sailing to wild cyclonic ones. I was enjoying the adventure of it, but the constant fever and flu like feelings I could well have done without. The trap door to the hull of the boat had been open and was half full of sardines. The fishermen were working hard to keep hauling in the nets which were straining under the weight of so many fish, threatening to break open before the catch was contained.

Pedro had his work cut out for him now as the ocean tossed the little boat from side to side violently on the dip and crest of the waves. We were over ten kilometres out on the Atlantic, a pawn in the hands of a violent storm with ice wind that seem to cut deep into my already inflamed chest. The fever had taken its toll and I passed out at the back of the boat, but the fisherman were far too busy with the heavy load of fish in the net to bother about me. Their attention was solely concentrated on opening the hull again to unload the haul into the hole with the rest of the catch. I opened my eyes long enough to feel the concerned Pedro lifting me up to be seated and taking his coat off, he placed it around my shoulders, then gently lay me on my side with an old fish smelling towel rolled up under my head. "Won't be long now," he said with his limited English vocabulary, "We'll be home soon and you be okay there." He pointed to the shoreline which could be seen now in the misty downpour. I nodded my head and slipped back into unconsciousness.

It was apparent upon later reflection that I had hit may head hard on the deck which resulted in hallucinatory visions of another life sometime in the future. In that state the bright lights of illumination touched my brain and I seemed to wake into a room of immense calm and natural clinical beauty. It was all white and it was all light. I was seated on a reclining chair with instruments everywhere, the equivalent of an emergency ward of a hospital, all protruding from the base of the chair that seems to be run by a multifunctional computer. I could see my own reflection, the chair, instruments and the computer with its array of flashing coloured lights; the only sterile objects that were not white in this room. Soft music was playing from somewhere that soothed my brain and calmed my body like deep meditation. The chair I sat in was opaque white and as I gazed down to where I sat I reexamined the reflection through an equally opaque wall and for an instant had an old biblical thought of "looking through a glass darkly." I seemed to be pinned down by two locking devises; brackets of clear glass. My restricted right wrist was facing upward, as a robot like arm from beneath the chair implanted a skin-like layer of thin plastic substance above my wrist, them a projected ray of light into my wrist caused immense pain but for a moment. That procedure over, a voice from beneath the chair spoke; "We have inserted your code number into your wrist now and it will serve to mark you forever more as the means by which you function in all things, of body, mind and spirit." I was given a choice to accept an algorithmic number selected by the computer or provide my own; I had chosen the latter.I knew that it would be easy to recall the number in case of an emergency, like a computer malfunction where I would be dependent upon the old ways, memory and paper transactions.

The number now implanted I had now joined the new agenda of the human race and was classed as 'a citizen of the earth.' Making my way from the government building that housed a central administration with its robots and computer controlled information, I appeared to be in a main street in a golden city were streets like transparent glass were laid out like a square of equal dimensions in height, length and width, and the thickness of the walls I noted were detailed in equal dimension being symbolic of the square root of the same, as of the 12 tribes of Israel and the 12 Apostles of Jesus, the Christ.

My brian was heralding a repetitive message that seemed of importance like in the Bible : 'And he causes all, both small and great, rich and poor, free and bond, to receive a mark in their right hand or on their foreheads; And that no man might buy or sell, save he that hath the mark, or the name of the beast, or the number of his name, Here is wisdom. Let him that hath understanding count the number of the beast: for it is the number of a man: and his number is 666." This revelation was not new to me but here I was having just received the barcoded number under my wrist aware that I now live in some future year. I perceived that I could not get by without the mark. For I sensed once I had come out of my hallucinatory state in the present moment that their was a prophetic message to be. I had been indoctrinated to it over the past three decades, slowly and surely by manipulation from trading in business, to banking and purchasing perceived needs of food, goods and services to maintain a way of life that over those years I reasoned was the only way to live life. Slowly but surely being absorbed into the use of mobile phones, computers and iPads and ultimately wifi iPhone watch for all of life functional requirements. So what was so different now? The Beast has had my profile unwittingly for years, as had government authorities, banks, the taxation department, social media, police and international security agencies as they have had on all of humanity in the western world. It was a much easier matter of convenience to do everything by simply a reading of my personal barcode on my wrist. At least that is how it initially seemed to me.

The Space Station satellite high above the earth was the receiving station that was programmed remotely from the earth sending stations which had and was still gathering all of humanities thoughts, words and deeds within its central memory and nervous system. Now the most powerful computer on earth at its central headquarters had control in a form of reverse osmosis were all the information, subject to manipulation had brain control mechanisms implanted within the barcode chip in the wrist or on the forehead of every living human and within the mechanics of the now advanced humanoid robot that had been built just before a pending Armageddon. The central nervous system of the computer brain at its whim activate signals to and from earth stations via its most powerful satellite signals from space to and from humans who had the computer chip barcode embedded under their skin. There being no more end to the aspects of our lives which could not be controlled- from birth control, to disease creation, war, death and destruction, programmed actions to create more 'problems' demanding solutions. The computerised system had the ability to take away free will and drive mankind to the dark side under the influence of an advance more powerful humanoid being who had created a robot society at its beck and call.

The risk far outweighed the convenience, when I sat down to look at the consequences of my acceptance of my implanted barcode. I had not considered this in this dream reality until after I had left the surgical centre where the skin implant had taken place. Now out in the new age world, I was facing a stark reality. I needed to know about this modern day society and the agenda of the Elite who controlled it all. I needed to clarify in my mind whilst I still had a remaining free-will, as to what this wrist band implant was really all about and why a central control body needed to know the deeper reasoning of my mind, the feelings of the heart and my spiritual agenda. The real reasons for the record keeping for all of mankind movements and personality traits was being held for no apparent reason. The system certainly had its positive benefits of convenient and easy to use of a barcode swipe by a laser light for the purpose of purchase of goods and services, for travel in driverless electric vehicles, for coming and go from public transport to international travel, but was there another agenda?

The Elite's misguided judgement of the ideal form of control via a microchipped population connected to a global computer was no longer a dream it was a reality. Individual and collective chipped messages of two way communication between the implanted brain of a computer once linked to the populous by the insertion of a 'link chip' of individual barcoded data signal to the brain of the central computer to and from the brain of humanity. A chip inserted on the wrist or forehead of humanity meant that there was no turning back and that there will be no end to the aspects of our lives which cannot be controlled- birth, to life and death. A living programmed system of actions and reactions to and from a central computer brain that could or would ultimate lead to a better life or an Armageddon.

There was so much to see and so much to investigate and learn about in this new strange world that I had entered, but it was not to be at this time for me. I was then drawn to a park like garden with many chairs an already there were people of various ages seated looking at a larger than life curtain of light above and my eyes without my control were drawn there too. I, like the others seated there, seem to be taken into a new state of consciousness and for the first time in my life I knew what it was like to have the other ninety percent of my brain being opened up to an enlightenment. I was seeing into the future, a newsreel like repeat of an immediate past. Above me a-visibility came into view that made things clearer now to me. My computer chipped programme had been tapped into the central computer of a network of clouds of information emitting from and two ever human being on earth including to and from me. It's was controlled via the central cloud computer known by humanity as 'the Beast' and the WiFi like signal of humanities thought processes were stored through it via the Space Station that had taken humanity's astronauts and scientists and engineers ten years to build. The Space station that could be seen from earth like a rising star in the north eastern sky every night reflection from the fading sun, arising to replace as it were the evening star, for it was much brighter. It had initially taken ten years to get the structure built and one hundred million dollar of sixteen participating nations, whose Astronauts lived up there in six months intervals whilst the network for 'The Beast' was being positioned. The Russians and the American working around the clock year round, supervising the whole structure whilst they lived up there. Sixteen nations working side by side under a united Russian- American alliance, building the project for 'The Beast' with their fellow nation participants. A goal of unity up there, whilst here on earth man fought for controlling territory as the Space Station project headed toward completion. Now it was all finished and the network of the beast used it as a beacon to signal humanities thought process via it from earth to the Space Station and back via the Cloud to the joint beast network of the matrix computer and humanity at large. All this now controlled via the man who worked the brain of the system known as the man of humanity, the one who humanity could, if they so desired from their enlighten brains use a process of algorithm to count the computer chip number of the beast, an ability that I as a prophet observer could now do. His number algorithmically was clear to me now, it being six hundred and threescore and six. He, the controller and power over the political, economic and religious of human society, and it under the new age of One World Order bearing the number 666. Whilst I had only just conclude that 666 had appointed himself the God of all, the Second Coming of Christ on Earth, worst of all, he believe it too. But it was not true, it was the greatest disception of all times of this New Enlightened Age.

Billions followed the controller's thought processes and gave all in homage to him, their mind, their body and their spirit as he so willed via the control process of the central computer known as 'The Beast'. This man who represented the thought processes of humanity was destined to destroy humanity in an Armageddon of evil that would be of unspeakable pain in their souls though processes in the eye of the storm. The man who repressed the all, the Christ controller who manipulates all was the one who had promised to return, for he was not the deceiver but the real one of combined unity of the souls of humanity. The new apostle beings who would give of their all in a dance of living unity would influence the Second Coming of the Christ who would defend those faithful descending upon 'a Cloud.' This Christ would bring humanity one thousand years of peace and the power of The Beast under the influence of the controller 666 would be extinguished for ten centuries. This would transpire until a finality of the world that we and future generations will come to know as the real end time.

The Master controller 666 manipulator of the system had begun to cause the Golden light city to be lowered to earth through his will and that of humanity as he prepared to enter a Temple of pure gold with streets like transparent glass, with walls thicker than any walls every built in the history of humanity, and this all being of humanities enlightened consciousness and will. For through humanity the Beast of our own existence, of our power and our will would bring death to billions of souls, through a reign of terror of those innocents who did not acknowledge this evil force within and those who did. We had still the free will to starve off this beast of burden 666 and embrace our collective inner consciousness of being, united as a force to be reckoned with, embracing the innocence and offer a new enlightenment consciousness for a Brave New World and not one governed by the evil of a hand in the dark of a One World Order. I look up with amazement, for this was a vision of immense beauty of a New Earth, like a template manifestation of the New Jerusalem, to come. A revelation in consummation God's people of group consciousness for the membership of dual citizenship with the God and mankind as one. It would be a renewed New Jerusalem of all God's people. That in reality would come into the hearts of man after the great and dreadful days of he who claimed his right of the beast, in the days to follow of dreadful Armageddon. It would be the end of earthly pilgrimage as we know it, as we the chosen people, the representation of the New Jerusalem of the people have a final and everlasting reconciliation in our hearts and souls, into what we might call a heavenly unity. It would be as was ordained; the City of God on this new earthly plain. A place free from terror and oppression and full of righteousness, a living temple in our own hearts. And it would come when we the people handed over all our self-will, body and soul, and what we thought we possessed in our advanced civilisation to the One true God, after the great and dreadful tribulations of Armageddon. The vision faded and I felt a dreadful pain in my right wrist where the barcode had been inserted and a sense of its removal was overcoming me. I had perceived the world over the coming decade was heading towards an Armageddon. I was not aware at the time that a Covid-19 virus would invade bringing humanity to a grinding halt. This would all end but felt sure that the Armageddon would take place in the form of war before the Beast had control. Before a New World Order became fully apparent and another catastrophic event would follow, a World War of Nuclear proportion causing the death of millions of humanity. It would be swift and sudden and pass as quickly as it came. Then the world would enter a new dimension of what I had perceived in my hallucinatory visions.

The last of my visions came as I slowly awakened to a conscious state of mind. I saw Jesus was walking by the sea of Galilee. The Apostle sat in a fishing boat not far from shore dejected as to their failure to catch a single fish when casting out their nets. The Christ man cried out to cast their net once more to the starboard side of the boat. They half heartedly cast their net and to their amazement caught a large haul of fish, so large that the net was at breaking point. It took all the fishermen's strength to drag the fish to the shore. On examination the fish were all of different species known to them. Jesus said "Come with me and I will make you fishers of men." As the vision faded I saw St. James the Apostle alone on the beach beckoning me to join him. In his hand he held a scollop shell. As he to faded from view I heard a lyric from my Santiago Traveller song," The symbol of the Camino, is but a scollop shell, the many roads maps on its back, many tails to tell; but when you turn it over, it turns into a hand, the one you recognise for our fellow man." The symbolism of these visions were not lost on me, for when I later evaluated their significance the boat repressed a City of God in which mankind could be as one. The fish, the different races of the world were in the hands of angelic guides within that city, and the fisherman the messengers calling all back to the way of the man from Galilee. St James appearance was a reminder of my having completed another Pilgrimage on the Camino de Santiago to return to the faith, the Church of my ancestors, the one I had in my adult life formally rejected.

GOD IS ALL YOU NEED.

"God is all you need,
 let nothing disturb you,
 nothing make you afraid.

 All things pass,
 God remains.

 Be patient,

 And you will attain your heart's desire.

 With God your own,
 you cannot lack,

 God Suffices.

 Amen"

\

CHAPTER 3.

IRISH LUCK

The rude awakening of what seemed immense pain had triggered me from my fevered body. Pedro, the Spanish fisherman of Finisterre, was leaning over me and like a skilled surgeon was removing a small fishing hook from beneath the skin of my right wrist with a pair of tweezers. It was apparent that I had this hook injected under my skin when I had fallen in a fever at the back of the fishing boat. My back-pack belongings were spread around me as Pedro removed the hook and laughed aloud. The wise old fishermen, knowing the nature of the Pilgrims of the Camino, had reasoned correctly that a well- travelled pilgrim would be carrying a medical kit in his back pack. Pedro, poured a little of the iodine from a bottle I had in my medical kit, found a band aid and placed it securely on the small wound. He then religiously repacked the iodine bottle and the tweezers in my medical kit and proceeded to repack it all in my back pack without as much as a word. The fever had broken and apart from a small bump on my head from the fall I felt much better. As I lay there on the deck of that fishing boat, gazing out to sea, with the last of the sun rays no longer visible re-placed by the clarity of a harvest moon, now shining like a pathway across the rise and fall of the swells of the impenetrable deep, I felt that I was free for the first time in my life. The vision I had experienced in my feverish unconsciousness, had enlightened me to my living in the now. A shooting star before my eyes flash across the sky like an omen of good things to come and burnt out just as quickly from the horizon beyond. A final curtain call at the end of a God given nature's day before a new dawning on the morrow and unknown journey awaited.

Leaving the fisherman attend to their nets, I thanked Pedro and made my way back through the charming twisting streets of Finisterre. Back to my private room overlooking the terracotta roofs of this cute little hideaway. I took a last glimpse of the village, the ocean and the sea of crystal stars on a blank of velvet sky and once more with my head upon my pillow, I drifted into a pleasant dream of astronauts, future beings and a crystal like Cathedral jewel in the great beyond. Awaken-ing with a slight headache from my fall and the weakness that always comes after fever, I quickly dressed and made my way back to a restaurant on the main Marina at the Finisterre harbour. The fisher-men's boats were already out at sea on their expedition to find another run of fish to catch. I mused at their way of life, those relaxed souls and thought of Pedro, his boat and a way of life that was his daily bread. I made my way back up the steep hill at the edge of town to the zero marker for a last view over Finisterre, the end of my Camino be-fore heading to my next adventure.

Many Pilgrims of The Way made it to the beach of Langosteria below me plunging into the ocean to purify their bodies and get rid of the dust from the road on their arrival at Finisterre. Others elected to follow the ritual of burning their clothing or throwing their walking boots into the ocean as a way of demonstrating letting go the material life to start a new life without things. My clothing for now and my boots I figured I still needed, as I had in my head a vision of more walking plans ahead in this hemisphere, before returning to my homeland down under. The view of the setting sun from Pedro's fishing boat the previous evening was a kind of death and the new day that had dawned a new beginning and a parting farewell to The Way, before I took flight to Ireland for my next stage of walking. The thoughts of my next Camino was overshadowed by the omen that arose before me. On the remains of an old ruin decayed wall, coming down the hill from the final zero marker of The Way, stood a painting of a Spanish musician dressed in traditional Irish folk dress, playing Irish Uilleann pipes; a timely omen as I made my way towards the road again, a return to Santiago for a flight to Dublin Ireland.

The Spanish customs officer rather annoyingly took my pocket knife from my luggage. I had travelled through Santiago airport twice with that knife before without so much as a hitch. I had declared it in my stored luggage on flights though French, Middle Eastern, Australian and New Zealand airports without so much as a glance at my luggage, but this time the customs guy at Santiago was adamant it was a 'weapon of Mass destruction.' He did not even enquire what I had used it for and may not have understood a pilgrim's viewpoint of the need of a knife as a sense of security and as a handy instrument to peel fruit or use to cut up a variety of eats at meal time. I fully understood his vigilance and strict viewpoint in an age of terrorism and found justification in the thought of good use of the knife over the years and the many kilometres of tramping this earth the knife has served me. It was no issue in purchasing another at my next port of call, so I contented myself with that evaluation and quietly handed the knife back to the Customs official.

The hostel Dublin, on a street with no name, with a black entry door, was a cheap and run down Refugio, as much for street people as the likes of me a Pilgrim off the road. Once I had booked in I wound my way up a couple of flights to a room with eight beds. Four by two double decker bunks with a bathroom facility and a wire cage locker draw that slid under the bunk for my back pack and clothing. As luck would have it I had a small lock and key in my backpack to secure my belongings. To be fair armed is to be forewarned I mused, with a flash of regret at the loss of my pocket knife. I managed to climb on board the remaining top bunk with the sheets supplied and made my bed. This was a much more tidy set up than most accommodation on the Camino Way where one had to side step other backpacks to make it to one's bed and nothing was secure. The inmates were quiet enough but the continual din from merry making and Irish music from a nearby pub was annoying. Next to my bunk a window overlooked a corrugated iron roof covered in cigarette butts, wet with a crop of moss that had probably not dried out ever, despite the current dry conditions. The bed was comfortable enough and I managed to sleep well throughout the night except for a rude awakening around 2.am. when two very drunk young Americans returned from their pub crawl. They and I settled down quickly and I noted as I drifted back to sleep that the pub downstairs was still in full swing and I could hear the sound of Irish bagpipes mixed with some frantic guitar playing and lots of drunken singing as I drifted back to sleep. Upon awakening at dawn, I quickly showered, dressed and had the free tea and toast on offer in the kitchen and made my way to the streets as a Dublin tourist. The noise of the night before had died down and all the pubs were closed. A few bleary eyed Irish were winding their way from a pub on a side street and Dublin was waking up again to a work day world.

An early morning visit to the national Cathedral was inspiring, having experienced the mystery of the middle ages Cathedral of Burgos and the glassed stained windows of light filled Leon Cathedral and the solemn majesty of the Cathedral de Santiago, with its famous St. James relics; Gothic arches and memorabilia of ancient days were not new to me. Except maybe for the spectacle of the 14th century replica of the tomb of Norman the Conqueror, the 'strong bow' of legends whose remains could not be sighted as they were kept in some chamber elsewhere inside the Cathedral and out of sight of tourists. It was possible, in certain hours of the day to walk the vast crypt running the length of the Cathedral building. It was built in the 13th century and housed many a saint's remains and Irish heroes of by gone days attracting the 'tourist' monies in preference to the pious reflections of those of us who preferred the sparse areas of God's Church instead of those of more maddening crowd variety. An oversized stained glass window of 'Strongbow' overshadowed an exhibition of 'Viking heritage' tracing the original invasion of the British Isles and the rudiments of the culture that still exists today. I took it all in as a good tourist must do. Making my way through the premier shopping location of the main thoroughfare to Grafton Street, I wound my way past buzzing cafes serving a late breakfast and observed women tourists taking in the latest fashions as they gazed into nearby shop windows. Here pubs were opening with patient patrons lounging around toughing it out for the first recovery drink to overcome the fog in their brains from the past night's hangover.

I backtracked along Grafton Street to St. Stephen's Green; a 22 acre Dublin's park, a gem and an oasis of calm, away from the hustle and bustle of the downtown city life. A quiet morning coffee and a stroll on the green grass through a flowered area, past an ornate fountain, over a bridge to feed ducks at a pond, as I watched children playing, full of laughter and carefree, it revived my flagging spirit. A nearby plaque of the 1916 Irish Uprising was a timely reminder of the waring nature within us all and the dreadful outcome of the battle that took place where I stood. This scene of combat was stopped, after an agreement from both sides that the battle would cease whilst the park keeper fed the ducks in the pond before the fighting proceeded. This 'cease fire' was possibly the best example to my mind of the power of nature and environment overruling the dark nature of man. The Easter week celebrations some 103 years ago was disrupted by a fight for Ireland's Independence in this park and throughout the streets of Dublin. I recalled that in 1916 the world recognized and remembered the 100th Anniversary of the Easter Rising, the rebellion for Irish independence that changed the course of Ireland's history when it began on the Easter Monday in 1916.

The seven members of the Irish Republican Brotherhood Military Council, comprising a writer, poet and schoolteacher, an ex-pat Scotsman who made Ireland his home, an English born American who had formally started the Brooklyn Gaelic Society, other Irishmen of American origin and a later President of Ireland. These seven Council members had declared themselves the "Provisional Government of the Irish Republic" and signed the Proclamation of the Irish Republic. The Proclamation itself outlined who was responsible for igniting the rising and referenced the Irish Republics alliance with Germany. These details of the proclamation, considered to be treason, ensured certain death by firing squad for the leaders if independence was not obtained. It is ironic now that over time the seven were executed and the North of Ireland does have its Independence whilst the south, being now more of an international cosmopolitan nature, is still a part of the British Commonwealth. At the height of the uprising, fierce fighting between the rebellious Irish and the British armed forces spilled into the streets of Dublin. With greater numbers and heavier weapons, the British Army suppressed the Rising. Of death and casualties, the Irish killed 143 British and the British army 66 of the rebels. Of the forces from both sides of that six day street fighting, there were 260 civilians killed and 2,217 civilians wounded and of the rebels, including their leaders, 16 were executed.

I ceased the reading of the plague in the St. Stephen's Green and the Irish Proclamation of the Republic at Easter 1916 and turned my thought back to the reality of the now. Apart from the 1916 Uprising, many a fine event had taken place in St. Stephens Green, not the least of which was an impromptu performance of Bono and U2 that had no-doubt encouraged them to enjoy the peace and quiet of the park too. With just one day stay in this fair city, I contented myself with winding my way along the River's edge, passing across many bridged thoroughfares that spanned the river Liffey from North to South. I did not have enough time to visit Trinity College to view the book of Kells, the books of Durrow and Armagh.

On reflection my time was limited in Dublin, so I decided to save that experience to another day, to revisit the land of my bloodline. Thinking I would stay another night in the city, I walked the way of the river in search of accomodation near O'Connell Street Station before catching a bus the next morning to start my walk on The Wicklow Way. Disoriented, I asked a passing Irishman for directions to O' Connell Street. He put down his brief case and with a wave of his hands began "Well, if you go down here a way." He pointed to the far off length of the straight line of street I was on, "then you turn left a few streets down, then you turn right and (pause) then again, I would not want to send you in the wrong direction." I thanked him for confusing me even further, so I decided to approach another: "Well" he said, "If you're going to O' Connell Street Station, I would not start here," but he did ultimately point me in the right direction. I was relieved to put down my back pack from my aching shoulder and in the foyer of my bedroom for the night rested my feet from the constant pounding of the pavement of the noisy city streets. The next morning I was up bright and early again to make it to the bus stop at the station for the next stage of my journey of life. The bus ride of some eighty kilometres out of Dublin had me arrive at Bunclody to a lively market centre. I satisfied my desired need to eat, as the fresh produce and sweet smells wafting from the market made me hungry. Satisfied now, I walked the Way from Bunclody to Shillelagh forest, to just out of town on the Wexford-Carlow border, where the rivers Slaney and Cloudy meet in the valley by the Backstairs mountains. Looking up to the distant Mt. Leinster, the highest peak standing sentinel, like a colossus overshadowing the valley floor below, I could see that I was in for a wonderful walk in the wood. An overnight stay in a B & B included a hearty breakfast which I enjoyed in the company of a chain smoking Dutch beauty, who happened to be staying in the nearby farmhouse, near the start of the walk. We made our way together on the Wicklow, following the Derry River then moving on to mixed forest trails below the summits of Uplands Hill, Moylisha and Raheenakit and reached the Stanakelly cross roads together.

It had been a pleasant laughing and sing-a-long day, alone with Josfie who, despite her ever present lighted cigarette hanging from her bottom lip, was grand company. We parted with a kiss on each cheek, but I felt that it was not the last of this Dutch beauty that I would see on the Wicklow. My overnight stay at a B & B on route had me seeking advice of the Way of the trek for this day. I had travelled some 26km with Josfie the day before and but a few kilometres on this cool fresh aired morn, I happened upon a landmark of an Irish pub, "The Dead Cow." A cosy little pub and a grand rest spot for a refreshing drink to further rest my aching limbs before tramping more of the Way of the Wicklow. I had agreed with the proprietor of the B & B that I would be staying another night and elected to do a loop walk for the day on an adjoining road to Moyne to look forward to hear more pub stories of adventure, of heroes and battles and Irish myths that reached back thousands of years, back to the ages of the Celts, the Viking Invasion and takeover of the Wicklow and even more myths of folklore and legends of Witches, Warlocks and War Lords! "Everything exists, everything is true, and the earth is only a little dust under our feet," I mouthed W.B. Yeats from his Celtic Twilight as I walked. He, like the characters of his tales, seem rooted in this kind of earth I now walked upon. A land filled with tales and epic characters that sent my imagination soaring.

The old boys in the "Dead Cow" 100 year old bar were telling their tales of yore over a Guinness or two, as I sat listening with quiet fascination. They were filling my head with other areas to walk in Ireland-The Giant Causeway, where Finn McCool and the Scottish Giant Benandonner dramatically fought each other. The Way of the Lover's Leap, along the Loop Head way in County Clare. It was there the mythical lovers Diarmuid and Grain jumped to safety after being pursued by an enemy army. The old men were roping me in to stay and do more walks in Ireland before I headed back home to Australia.The locals were keen for me to stay and walk the ancient Lia Fail, Ireland's Stone of Destiny, at the hill of Tara in County Meath. The stone that had such mythical magic for the Irish was thought to be brought back from the underworld by the god-like Tuatara De Danann. It reminded me of similar stories of ancient stones of Australian aboriginal myth and those of the New Zealand Maori. Like those legends the mystical stone had shouted out when the true King of Ireland touched it. The old boys continued with stories of Halloween in Ireland's Celtic past and the division between this world and the otherworld being so thin that spirits could pass to and from without too much of an issue. They reminded me of the deep hole of Oweynagat- in the Cave of Cats-in County Roscommon, where the large stone boulder that topped it was once thought to be the opening door to the otherworld. I thanked my hosts at the little bar of the 'Dead Cow' and made my way back on the Wicklow Way. Perhaps I would return to fit the 40,000 ring forts that doted the landscape-visit the ancient structures as I had done in Portugal in my 2015 Camino form Lisbon to Santiago.

Unlike the ancient Romans and the hunter gatherers of Portugal history and of the Australian Aboriginal and New Zealand Maori, the Irish added a different dimension to their mythical story telling; that of Christian and Pagan superstition, of little bearded men, leprechauns being the most common of them all. I mused over the stories they had told me and the many more that I had discovered in my research. I was returning to my family roots in Ireland but knew I had the challenges now that lay ahead for me on the Wicklow Way. The Wicklow links to the early Vikings, a faint sniff of my Spain Camino's, the Uilleann pipes and 'the end of the earth' at Finisterre and a mythical story of a map depicting a Mahogany Caravel sailing ship in some monastery on the Way attracted me like a magnet to the walk. There were rumours also of the early Spanish fisherman visits to the Wicklow, so it was in my DNA to make this journey of what I might call my Irish Camino Way. None of it came true of course but it seemed good reason at the time to venture there.

On the road again the next morning, I passed the turn to Shillelagh through the forest of the same name, where the story of a great battle between Viking pagan and invading Christians had long ago taken place. I was reminded of the history of the place upon sighting a massive fine oak tree. The "Shillelagh' folklore of a short, stubby blackthorn cudgel known as an ancient Irish shilled laugh was not traditionally of Ireland but rather a badge of honour for many skilled fighter in historic ancient battles. It was a very popular weapon in 19th century London, used mainly as a fighting stick between opposing street gangs. It later become a popular walking stick and weapon against being attacked by wild dogs or villainous thieves on a walk through back streets of towns or country road.

The name 'Shillelagh' or 'Sham' gets its name in Ireland from the Gaelic 'bara'- which means, fighting stick- the original cane gets its Irish name from the Shillelagh Forest into which I found myself walking. The massive fine old oak tree I passed was the area where the forest here was famous for many a massive oak. Sadly, most of them were cut down and exported. It was of little comfort to me knowing that famous buildings throughout Europe were built with imported Irish oak. Thinking of the Irish woodwork of Westminster Hall, I recalled the description of the mansion in Banim's 'The Croppy': "solidly wainscoted with Shillelagh oak against the venomous spider of England durst not affix his web." When Irish boys come of age, they were exposed to the tradition of the 'bata' and carried a stick as a rite of passage into manhood. Many a young Irishman practiced with a 'bata stick' used in sparring that was needed to improve their skills. Whilst father's taught their sons to always hold the 'bata' tightly to the chest so as never to be taken unawares, the finer points of use were taught by a fencing master. Whilst the stick was carried by Irishman just about everywhere they went, it was at festivals, wakes or Saint's feast days that it was needed the most. Factions were always present at most social gatherings and fighting was very common until the famines of the 1840s. Most often the faction fighters were members of certain families or political groups. Sometimes the fighting would consist of hundreds of men welding their Shillelagh bata. The knob on one end was hollowed out and filled with molten lead; this was known as a 'loaded stick.' it was not necessary to 'load' the root of a blackthorn because it could pack a significant whack in any case.

My mind was recalling the story of how Wicklow got its name. When Christianity won the day in battle over the residing Viking, it was here that one of St. Patrick's 'fighting' priest returned to the Shillelagh to establish the Church and he was given the name 'Wicklow' by the locals after he had his teeth knocked out in battle. The name Wicklow in Gaelic means 'the toothless one!' I wound my way along a country road and up a mountain track with fantastic views over the lush countryside to another mountain track along the Muskeagh Hill. Leaving the trail near Ballycumber lane, I discovered the remnants of an old ringed fort and a present reminder of the constant enemy that those early inhabitants of this area had to face. The road twisted and turned in different directions through forests and across country lanes and I realised I had lost my bearings and had no compass as a guiding light. Arriving at a crossroad I elected to toss a coin to determine a choice of walking left or right and concluded a good omen on the result of a 'tail'! Turning left on the toss, I made my way for about one kilometre and down a hill I came across a cottage. Outside in a small garden sat a man of about my age sitting smoking a pipe, taking in the pleasure of the warm sunshine on his lily whites with his shirt off. Between puffs of smoke he consumed what seem to be a pale ale. When he spotted me approaching, he quickly got of the chair and wandered to his front fence to greet me. The wife appeared at the door off the cottage with a glass of water in hand and motioned me to drink.

The old timer was more interested in my story and where I was bound. Eventually, after a lengthy chat, we got around to directions and I mentioned that I knew my way back to where I was staying, if he could point me in the direction of the 'Dead Cow' pub, I would make my way from there. He immediately went into a long citation of the little pub's history and how it had become his competition. It seems he brewed his own booze and was in direct competition to the little pub. The "Dead Cow" had been in the same family for over one hundred years and all male members had a direct link also to representing Ireland in the game of Rugby. The tiny little one bar pub had a wall full of family Rugby photos and I longed to know more but declined from pursuing that line for fear that would get meon the booze myself if I spent too much time there.

The old man at the fence asked me if I would like to taste his brew and so that he was not offended, I explained that I was an alcoholic. Leaving the old guy at the fence waving goodbye and thanking his good wife for the drink of water I made my way back to the "Dead Cow." Matt, the proprietor, after I consumed a refreshing soda, offered to take me to another departure point along the Way of the Wicklow in the morning. So I stayed the night listening to his stories. I had no urgent agenda to hurry my tramping of the Wicklow, and was keen to hear more of Matt's stories. Matt, like most with Irish blood including myself, loved telling stories. Matt's pet topic was of ghosts, dark spirits of bye gone days and weird events surrounding relatives, living and dead. In one of his stories Matt described a haunted house were his sister and brother in-law lived. It was a common practice for his kin to play the Ouija board for fun, knowing that it was a traditional parlour game of historic bar drinking time wasting and unrelated to the occult. That is until an American Pearl Curran popularised its use as a divining tool during World War 1.

The fun for Matt's sister and brother in law went wobbly when they made the mistake of not heading the warnings when playing the board, that both occultists and Christians alike warned against; the practice of calling upon spirits of the dead. The simple innocence and mystical minds of many Irish fall for the trap of believing in their own bull shit. So Matt's brother's request to test the theory, called for a visit from a spirit of the past of a dead family relative who had passed over in the home they occupied. Well, being under the same roof of their long departed relative, it was a might too far to go on the Ouija board. No sooner had they completed the game and were heading to bed when a strange smell and happening occurred. Apparently the floor boards and entry carpet to the cottage accumulated a vast amount of dust. The body of dust continued all the way up the staircase to their adjoining bedroom and a dank smell emanated. They both tried to open that bedroom door but it proved too difficult, as if someone was holding the door closed from inside the room. They finally managed to release the door the next morning and dust was thick in the air and all over the bed and the furniture. It did not matter how many times the two Ouija board players, cleaned up the rooms, the staircase and entry to front door foyer, the dust reappeared. In desperation Matt's brother called in the local priest who did his best to try exorcism of the spirit who emitted the dust, but had no such luck, as the dust just keep reappearing night after night. In desperation they called in a medium who entered the bedroom, producing a piece of rope and watched it as it went wildly dancing around the room.

Realising that there was a force linked to the dead relative who had apparently died in that room, the medium began to question the living relation of the one long past. He enquired as to what they had both been doing differently before the dust happening had first occurred. The Medium soon discovered their nightly ritual of play with the Ouija board and the calling on the spirits of family past. Rather annoyed that such amateurs were playing with the occult so blatantly, the medium gave them a good lecture and made them promise never to play the board game again. He returned to the bedroom, staircase and down stairs entry foyer and performed an exorcism in each of those areas of the house. Matt's brother at the bequest of the exorcist left with the Ouija board tucked under his arm and Matt's sister and brother in law's lives return to normal. Matt was on a role now with family historic happenings and after a couple of more drinks, related the story off his Aunt May who lived in a dark house without electricity, her only source of light being from an open fire . Aunt May used a bellows to fan the flames to keep her light burning bright. She was a strange one. Matt exclaimed; only ever wearing dark slacks, a heavy dark coat in winter and a dark cloak over her head, Matt was sure she was a Witch. She lived quite alone apart from a ginger cat with one black patch over its right eye and a mean smile like a tiger on its lips. When Aunty May occasionally took off the hood that covered her face, Matt said she had the most beautiful blue eyes and a permanent smile on her lips. Apart from her strange habit of dressing in black and staying indoors, she had a happy knack of predicting good fortune with accuracy and was always very kind to small children. I was ready for bed after a long day but Matt insisted that he had a further surprise for me and he interrupted his story telling me to fetch a small torchlight and his car keys. I piled into the back of his car in the dead of night, with his wife Ann and a little Scottish terrier for company. Matt had a plan of that I was sure, and he was gearing me up for a crescendo for the evening. We left the village along a winding dirt track and Matt began to tell a more gruesome tale. Apparently it had been on the evening news a day or two back, where a Dublin man had killed his mother in law and her body parts had been found in the Wicklow Mountains.

Matt hastened to tell me that her body parts were found in the forest of the mountain track I was to walk the very next day. Apparently, the murderer had been arguing with his mother in law and stabbed her to death in a fit of rage, initially buried her body in the backyard of her home. The news report had advised that he had later returned to the home, apparently afraid that the body might be discovered. He had dug her up, cut her into small pieces and even skinned the back bone off her carcass and put all into plastic bags, distributing the remains in the Wicklow Mountains close to the track I was to walk upon the next morning. The forensic scientist had advise the police that the method used by the killer to cut up the body had to be the precise work of someone who was very skilled with using a knife.

It turned out the killer's occupation was a butcher and had no issue with cutting up the body. Matt explained how the body parts were discovered within twenty four hours after the killer scattered them off the trail, deep in the forest foothills of the Wicklow Mountains.The killer was hoping the body would be eaten by birds of prey and the bones taken by wild dogs to chew on. The prospects of discovering her re mains was remote, or so he thought. By chance, some bush walkers, within days of the killer's actions, had parked their car in a remote car park not far from the forest track where the remains of the women had been scattered. They had been walking in the forest and upon return-ing to their car discovered that thieves had broken in and stolen some personal possessions. Not content to just report the matter to the po-lice they began scouring the forest floor in the hope of finding some of the things that had been taken. It was there on the forest floor they discovered the severed head of the killer's mother-in-law.

The clue to the location of her body parts was advised to police by the killer, who whilst under interrogation indicated all would be found near a waterfall just off the Wicklow mountain track. I cursed that Matt had told me of this news, as I would be walking near those very falls the very next day. Matt drove us to a remote village where we roamed quietly through what was once a school for local village children. A church still standing by the side of the old stone-made school was much worse for wear as it was in decay from lack of use as much as from the elements. A cemetery which housed the remains of the late sole school teacher stood nearby. Apparently he had lived at the back of the church in a small room which was still standing, well preserved except for a missing door and roof. The vista was over 200 years old and the children of the school, the church, like the teacher and part time preacher, had long ago passed on.

Matt stood in admiration of the historic place, off the beaten track and although it had long ago lost its usefulness as hallowed ground for the education of children in matters of life, the world and the church, it was altogether historic for me too. Matt had a last glance back at the sight and made a last comment as we drove off. "Isn't it grand" he said. I agreed but was more fascinated by the old decayed bank across the track and the supply store that stood nearby that had once been the centre of a commercial community. Matt wound the car along another rough track until we came across an ancient ruin known as 'the place of Rings.' This area had been a Viking settlement and whilst no buildings remained, some stone outer walls of a compound looking over a field still stood. In the background a moat and a large thick wall on level ground indicated a central compound had once been there. No doubt a vantage point for tribal leaders and foot soldiers overlook-ing the villagers and oncoming enemy. It was pitch black as we won-dered around aimlessly in the dead of night, blind save for a constellation of stars above to guide our way. Although it seem well past my bedtime, Matt insisted we move to another sight that he wanted to show me before the night was over. Our final port of call was an original church ruin built by the first priest himself. I could almost hear Wicklow's footsteps on the stony entrance to the door of the church ruin and see the smile on the face of the old 'toothless' priest. It had been a long day's journey into night and I was feeling very weary given that I had walked a long way apart from Matt's ghostly mystical tour, but I would not have missed it for quids, the tales of myth and the local folk's legends. Awakening from a night of dreaming of ghosts, witches, warlocks and the presence of 'Father Wicklow' in deep conversation with the Viking warrior 'Strongbow.' I made my way to the kitchen for breakfast before heading out on The Wicklow again. Matt had breakfast prepared for me and was cleaning up the dog shit from the kitchen floor with an evil eye planted on his sorrowful dog hiding in his sleeping basket in the corner. "You little fucker" he exclaimed and the dog put its cute head down and glanced up from the top of his basket bed with a peering knowing and guilty look. After I settled up my account, I gathered my belongings and heading for the door to make my way to the mountain track. Matt dutifully handed me a brown paper bag with my lunch pre-packed and would not accept any money from me for the contents. Anne, the always thoughtful wife, had prepared lunch for me to sustain me for the day ahead. I almost felt like a school kid again, heading off with my lunch and school pack.

CHAPTER 4.

GHOSTS OF HILL AND DALE

The terrain of the Wicklow changed to forest paths and challenging hills which thankfully were not wet and muddy, for it had not rained there for over two weeks. My conversation with the local old distiller of whisky the day before, confirmed this fact adding that the local farmers were concerned with the lack of rainfall. The river beds dried up quickly on The Wicklow and two weeks was almost considered a drought. I thought of the farmers and graziers at home in the bush, a couple of years of drought could be tolerated but our droughts in Australia have been known to last longer than that. Whilst I felt for the farmers in the Wicklow Valley, I was personally thankful for the dry earth beneath my feet and the sunshine of the morning. I could still hear Matt's parting words as I waved him farewell. "I wish you a long and happy life Doug, where everything is grand for you." It seems like everything was always 'grand' for Matt, be that having a drink, a chat, examining gravestones at night or telling mythical tales of the past. I was already missing that big friendly bear of an Irishman. The climb into the forest was challenging as I started to gain altitude but the effort was worth it to view the stunning mountain scenery on the foothills of the Wicklow Mountains. My mood was somewhat sad with thoughts of the scattered remains of a dead mother-in-law that only recent lay close to path I walked upon. I heard the sound of the waterfall as I climbed; it was where the killer had disposed of the woman's body and even sliced the flesh of her spine. "Sick Fuck" I had exclaimed aloud, and almost in the same breath said,"Sorry Lord." Quickly, I galvanised my thoughts, focusing on the steep ascents that I was then engaged in. Coming to a clearing in the forest at the peak, I got my first glimpse of Lugnaquilla, the tallest mountain in Leinster, on the Wicklow Mountain range.

Continuing to climb even further along the trail to Carrickashane Woods, I reached a clearing for a better view of the Lugnaquilla from its south prism side. There was a mist hiding the mountain as I reached my zenith and my mind said "But it isn't there," I knew it was but it did not appear to be so. Then the mist lifted and it was there, beyond time, before space, close, alive, huge beyond any scale of comparison. Eternal silence, motionless power, being a perfect presence. I had climbed many a mountain range mush higher and immense but this was different. There was something strange how the mist had lifted and there it stood, it was stunning and immense in its ghostly reality. I wanted to be one of its mountaineers during the winter months of moisture rich muddy soil freeze, allowing me to climb like one would a frozen waterfall in Scotland or a glacier in New Zealand. It was a long hard beautiful day for future memory recall of a mountain I probably would not ever climb. My 21 km journey, moving down from the heights and into the valley below. The journey down the steep mountain slope was at jogging speed as I entered another evergreen forest, descending even further into the Glenmalure valley, I walked at a slow pace then to a cosy fireside log cabin, my home for the night.

My morning breakfast was delivered with a pleasant surprise; Josfie, the chain smoking blond beauty from Holland made her way to my table and we exchanged our days news thus far on own spirited journey. As it transpired she was only a few kilometres ahead of me for the whole of the previous day and it was by sheer chance that if I had stayed so long at the top of the forest gazing at the Lugnaquilla mountain, I would have easily caught up to her. We ate an enjoyable breakfast together and I waited until she smoked her first cigarette for the day, before we shouldered our backpacks and made our way onto the U -shaped glacial valley of Glenmalure glaziers, but a short 14 km to Glendalough and as we gained altitude shaking off the feeling of a valley floor, we returned to more spectacular scenery of the Wicklow Mountains. Together with laughter and a sing along of my ever present 'Walking the Camino' song, Jofsie sang along like so many Pilgrims had done with me on my Camino de Santiago, asking me to sing it again as it seemed to lift her spirit.

 Along the way we were met by Karen, a Canadian middle aged animal farmer, who talked continuously about horses, sheep and cattle. The cow girl had red hair, freckled face and rough hands and equally rough handshake, but there was a certain charm about her disposition and an unusual exceptional bubbling personality. We stopped to pat some donkeys grazing near a fence and whilst Josfie and I stroked the coat, mane and nose; Karen was busying herself embracing them and kissed them on the nose. We had time to spare and would easily make Glendalough by nightfall, so we left the donkeys and our track to explore the heart of The Wicklow Mountains National Park. We could see the 6th Century Monastic village of Glendalough a few kilometres ahead, so we decide to rest a while near the lake and do a little exploring of the 8th Century village that we had come across. The Glendalough hotel and accommodation facilities were just around the corner so to speak. Well in fact it was a couple of kilometres from the 8th Century 36 metre tower we had come across and could be viewed from across a river running into an estuary that flowed from a glacier. It was a beautiful site but the tower was long past carrying the weight of humanity as a looout point. The primary historic function of the Tower was that of a belfry- the annals almost always labeled it as a bell house. The traditional use of the round tower, taught to past generations, was one of defence, particularly during Viking raids on the nearby monastery and church facilities. It served now to be a hotel and resort like accommodation facility. It is said that it was used for temporary refuge during sudden Viking attacks. Maybe true and maybe not as such free standing round towers of uniquely Irish architecture tower elsewhere had survived were-as similar towers in Ireland have not. The towers were more importantly symbols of prestige, power and wealth, and not of the ecclesiastical community that built them but more of their patrons.

Apart from the use as a bell tower and a place of refuge during Viking attacks it may have acted as a treasure house.The large second floor windows may have well allowed relics to be displayed. A typical use being the scriptoria of monk's writings, copied and displayed in the windows as illuminated manuscripts. They were considered sacred places but I thought as I gazed upon this relic of a past life, that one may never know of its real function. Nearby the 12th Century abandoned lead and zinc mine and the eerie St. Saviour's priory were all explored by us before we settled down to conversation over dinner at the resort hotel complex- a far cry from the B & B' s we had experienced along the Wicklow way. I fell asleep with the message of a final Biblical quote embedded in my brain: "Fear God and keep his commandments, for this is the whole duty of man. For God will bring every deed into judgement including every hidden thing, be it evil or good."
With the merriment of the evening meal, drinks and good conversation behind me, I drifted into sleep with yet another quote as to the measurement of human life's benefit, Ecclesiastics came to mind: "Good wine, good food in the pleasant company of friends, offering it all to God." My lips spoke to the darkness, "What more could one man want, what greater benefit can one man receive?"The next morning we had a late breakfast together, Josfie, the chain smoking Dutch women and Karen, the Canadian horse lover and me, the happy writer of verse and singer of songs, happy travellers on our individual pathways and before the day turned to night again, maybe destined to part from this brief time together and possibly never to see each other again in this lifetime. Life can be like that I thought, with all our comings and goings, people pass through our lives over time like ships in the night. We explored the 6th century village of Glendalough which was once referred to as the centre of learning in Europe and took a last look at the old Tower walls and abandoned mine shaft before getting back on the way again. After a twelve kilometre exhaustive climb, I headed off to Roundwood, some fifteen kilometres away.The past days had been pleasant in the company of a cigarettes smoking Josfie and 'donkey hugging' Karen, but it was time for parting, as we had made good time to where the trail skirted the village of Laragh.

We had walked a mix of peaceful forests trails together, over mountain paths and valley floors. We said our farewells with final hugs and kisses and a sense of sad parting. I stepped off the Wicklow Way to explore the lively village of Laragh with its shops, restaurants and bars before heading off to Roundwood. I had come to feel the comfort of tramping with them both, but like me they were tramping on their own path of homely happy destiny. Josfie was getting over a long standing love affair back in Holland and Karen had recently divorce and I could resonate with their pilgrimage on the Wicklow. "All good things pass in time," I said to myself as I made my way on a rather dangerous road to the outskirts of Roundwood where I stopped for a bite to eat at a pub on the edge of town.

It was late morning when I arrived at "The Wicklow Heather" and I was relieved to rid myself of the burden of my backpack and getting off that busy road. It had been a narrow main road I had walked for the past eleven kilometres and I had to move closer to the edge of the embankments with every step and every passing car. I made enquires with the proprietor of the pub to secure accommodation at a nearby B & B and the barman explained that the owner was an hour away and my accommodation was three kilometres on the way out of town. He assured me that my room was available and that it was best to wait and relax, either at the bar or in the restaurant area. So I settled into the restaurant to what was a typical pub meal of roast beef, vegetables and a pile of mashed potatoes. I was content to wait patiently and once satisfied with a full stomach, I made my way to the next room to visit a surprising museum of past geniuses. It was called 'The Author's room' and housed many photos and memorabilia of famous Irish authors and stockpiles of their notable works. James Joyce's 'Portrait of an Artist as a young man' caught my eye as did his 'The Dubliners' and his much more well known 'Ulysses.'

With another rendition of L.Cohen's "Hallelujah" wafting from the adjoining bar and ringing in my ears almost like elevator music to me I was seeking change. I had heard it repeatedly on all of my former Camino walks, and was pleased to retreat into the silence of the Author's room and visits the ghosts of Irish past. Every wall and cabinet had a photo and synopsis on a series of plaques of the most famous of authors and what may well have been the original copies of their words in glass cases held under lock and key. The appearance of Wilde, Kavanagh, O' Casey, Brian and Yeats captured my attention and my exploration for this wondrous collection of their history and memorabilia had me engrossed. I was glued to the tributes to each author when suddenly interrupted by the barman. He advised me that the boss could not make it back for a while longer and he would act as my taxi service from now on and that I could settle my drinks, meal and accommodation bills in the morning. I reluctantly left the Author's room resolved to return their after my morning breakfast for further exploration. The barman returned at a prearranged time to transport me back to the pub and I settled my bill and returned to join the ghosts of the past in the author's room, viewing the portraits and the written words of the plaques even more closely than the previous day. I was glued to the tributes to the authors and their detailed real life experiences outside their written masterpiece. They were all damaged souls and I felt an affinity with their humanity as well as their words. I knew so much how letting go with writing a journal, a poem or writing a story meant to me in my own damaged self- esteem, It was perhaps the only real way outside of drinking oneself to death or handing the head over to a professional head shrink, that one could attain peace of mind. The morning was warming up and I took one last glance over my shoulder at "The Wicklow Heather' before shouldering my backpack for my next port of call at Enniskerry, some nineteen kilometres away. Making my way off the beaten path up a bush track, I climbed a nearby hill for one last look over the Glendalough and the lagoon in the distant valley below. It called for a poem to write down my thoughts of the pub and my find of the Author's room. I was in a vacant and pensive mood as I wandered down the hill and back on to the track of the Wicklow.

No more than two kilometres out of Roundwood I came to an intersection in the road which led me to a spectacular section of the Wicklow. The Way took me across mountain tops with the distant views of both mountains and coastline. Thankful that there was hardly a cloud in the sky, as I ascended a ridge, crossing a historic bridge with a fast flowing stream below me. I made my way up another steep climb to the ridge around Lough Dan to look down on the location where both the TV series " The Vikings' and Mel Gibson's 'Braveheart' were filmed. A little further on I discovered a perfect vantage point to view Lech Toy, a dark brown lake flanked by a white sandy beach. It resembled a pint of Guinness, and reminded me of the pleasure of drinking that fluid, partaking of the rich dark fluid with the foaming white top. I cast the thought out of my alcoholic brain and headed north through a forest. I was joined there by a couple of young Irish girls out for a day's tramp together. It began to rain a mist as we traversed a narrow ridge together and the girls were concerned they would get soaking wet as they had no wet weather gear with them to protect against the elements. I had experience enough of the weather conditions on the Wicklow to assure them that it was not going to actually rain, it was just a mist and it would pass soon. Not long after I had made this prediction, we descended another steep slope and the mist faded with every step and back into pure sunlight again. The girls were walking faster now and I let them get far ahead as I needed the time alone to contemplate and focus on the dangers of a mishap and fall. I was thankful for the whole week on the Wicklow that it didn't rain once and thought again of the disappointment of the farmers of The Way. Walking onward to the 'Djouce'- Wicklow's best known mountain, I descended to see the powerhouse and distant waterfall. It was to be the end of my Wicklow walk, as I had made my pre- booked accommodation at the "Coach House" in the Glencree valley township. I ended my walk with happy thoughts, enjoying another pub meal.

It was a little way to the exit to catch the bus to Dublin, so I walked a final track of the Wicklow over a mountain top and along another forest track, climbing another mountain to see the city of Dublin come into a view as I arrived at a cairn where a stack of two big stones at what is known as two rocks marked my timely end to the Wicklow Way mountains. I took one last look at the Dublin city skycap and the impressive panorama of the bay before making my way to a Georgian estate at Marly Park for the finish line. I stayed the night there, had a sleep in, a full breakfast and caught the bus back to O' Connell Street station for my next port of call, Galway.

The Wicklow Way.

It was on the Wicklow trail,
I stopped to make a stand
put down my backpack upon the track
took pen and paper in hand.

The morning t'was bright with sunshine
the air was crisp and clear
I had no reason for my pensive mood
just let me make that clear.

So I sat on a rock
overlooking the valley below
Glendalough not far away
vacant thoughts began to flow.

My pack was too great a burden
the sun was getting hot
I could see no reason for my way
the road was hard enough.

It seemed I'd lost my mojo
had nothing to sing about
so I stopped at the " Wicklow Heather"
for breakfast and a tea.

It was at that place near Glendalough
upon the Wicklow Way
I'd put down my back pack burden
weary and hungry.

The room was dark and ghost like
so I just ventured on in
but not before I finished
my breakfast and that tea.

The room was lit with memories
many books there to see
ghostly photos of past authors
and faded memories.

There was Wilde and Joyce
Kavanagh and Durcan
O'Casey and Behan
Herein their thoughts still rang.

There was Yeats and Synge'
Heaney and many more
and over in a corner
George Bernard Shaw.

There were so many old books
dusty by the door
photos of ghosts from the past
where memories lingered more.
So I stayed with them awhile
their words were clinging to me
but I had to leave regrettably
I was busting for a pee!

Once more on the Wicklow Way
I climbed a nearby hill
gazing down upon the lure
of Glendalugh's past still.

There I sat upon a rock
dead poets in my mind
wise words written by long gone authors
some for reason, some that rhyme..

Oh! I carry my books for insurance
CDs of songs that I wrote
singing a line or two of my rhythm
if they fork some lightning.

If you see me tramping on some foreign shore
with a burden on my back
just stop and say " Buen Camino"
and I'll shout "Buen Camino" right back!

Now I'm happy to sell you a book or a song
to relieve my aching back
in fact you can have the blooming lot
just for a few Euros at that!

But I won't sell you my back pack
it carries my sleeping sack
nor the food that I need for my journey ahead
I'll not be selling you that!

And so my Wicklow Way had come to its demise, and I got to thinking of my next port of call and an old song of Bing Crosby came to
mind.

"With a shillelagh under me arm
And a twinkle in me eye
I'll be off to Tipperary in the morning
With a shillelagh under me arm
And a toohra loora lie
I'll be welcome in the land that I was born in.

Me mother told the neighbours
I'm going to settle down
Phil the fluters coming out
to play me round the town

And with a shillelagh under me arm
a twinkle in my eye
and a tooth loot lie
I'll be off to Tipperary in the morning.

Pat McCarthy's going to have
a party Saturday night
I'll be there with my bejabers
cause there is bound to be a fight.

With me shillelagh under me arm
And a toohra loora lie
I'll be off to Tipperary in the morning."

CHAPTER 5.

MORE IRISH LUCK

The fast train to Galway from Dublin took around five hours. It rained heavy on my arrival and it rained for the remaining days upon my journeys in Ireland. I happily flagged down a taxi for a trip to the sea-side of Galway Bay. I could have easily walked it but the rain was just too heavy and my chest ached with the cold and flu symptoms. I quickly found a B & B in the heart of Galway township, showered and got into some fresh clothing and after doing my washing I made it to the street and a local laundry service to use the dryer. Not far from the main corner to the bay front I visited the Catholic church for a quiet meditation whilst my clothing was drying and then a walk to a nearby pub for an early evening meal. I noted on the T.V that the British Isles were playing the New Zealand All Blacks at 8.A.M. the following morning and the pub would be opened for breakfast for those keen enough to watch the game. I had decided then and there to have an early night and have breakfast at the pub in the morning to watch the match before venturing out to walk Galway Bay.

Awakened early by the call of nature and the thoughts of a grand Rugby match, I showered again and headed across the road for breakfast to await the T.V reception. The room was crowded with enthusiastic Irish spectators already drinking Guinness and getting charged up for the game. I must have looked a sight to them as I ate my bacon and eggs and drank a pot of tea seated in the front row at a table near the T.V. set waiting for the game to start. It was a cracker of a game and I was the ' foreigner from down under,' the closest target to New Zealand for the Irish drinking spectators that morning and for the first time in my life I prayed the New Zealanders would get beaten so that I didn't. To make matters worse the Captain of the Lions was a local Irish lad, a 24 year old Peter O'Mahony, who had become the 11th Irish Captain of the British lions in the history of the touring side. Looking back on it now, that cracker of a game, the Irishmen in the pub that morning were arguably just as dedicated as I was to the game of Rugby. I thanked God that there were no Shille-lagh sticks among the boisterous rabble as they got more verbose with angry venom cast at the Australian referee's decisions during that match. Being the close representative of Australia, I breathed a sigh of relief paid my bill and left the pub after the match without my blood being spilt. My days of bar room brawls far behind me after giving top the booze. I was chuffed that New Zealanders won the match and it was another memorial event for a Rugby tragic. It was a couple of matches too soon for me to be in that bar on that morning as the Irish went on to win the series on their New Zealand tour. It was the first time the All Blacks had been beaten on home soil in many a long day.

Making my way along the broad walk and taking in the scenery of the carnival atmosphere of Galway Bay, I was soon joined by an Irishman of my own age and eager for a chat. We walked along the Bay fore-shores talking about the weather which is always a good starting point in Galway were it rains more than it shines. The weather on this day was initially fine although Tom the Irishman talked up a storm when I mentioned I had been to Fatima on my 2015 Camino. He told me in his beautiful Irish brogue of his experiences with Fatima and it was from him that I learnt of the bullet that almost killed the Pope in 1961. The bullet being now housed in the crown of the statue of Mary at Fatima. The same statue that was built in 1921 over the spot were the children had experienced the apparition of Mary in 1917. Tom also gave me an Irish history lesson on St. Patrick; the dear old Saint of the Isle. St .Patrick had been born in Britannia, an area of the isle once governed by the a seperate kingdom before James IV of Scotland became King of England and Ireland.

According to Tom, the details of St. Patrick's birth were in county Mayo and I made a mental note to look up those details when I returned to Ireland and on to Mayo were my grandmother was born. My Grandfather being born a little further north and more centre of Ireland in County Cavern. Patrick, a devout Catholic priest, in order to explain the Trinity of the Father, Son and Holy Spirit, used a three leaf clover to demonstrate the three persons in one God theory. A concert granted to those early Irish Christians who listened to Patrick preaching and to those who practiced the Catholic faith today. That he drove snakes from the emerald Isle is a myth well used with effect by those who wanted to believe in something. St. Patrick's reportedly drove pagan Celtic worshippers out of Ireland and demonic spirits from 'suffering sinners' with the use of a banner with a snake head as a catalytic brand to emphasise his point. This may all be just myth too as he originally came from Wales, and spent many a night and day on the high seas. He could have seen many a snake sliding into the ocean into more warmer currents than in Ireland, where the water temperatures is always very cold. In fact New Zealand ocean currents are on par and there are no snakes there either. It is presumed Patrick used the snake symbol which depicts Mary, Mother of Jesus, crushing the head of the serpent and this symbol is also depicted in many historic paintings and icons throughout the Christian world. The celebration of St. Patrick's day was traditional to help to commemorate Patrick's success in the removal of Celtic pagans from Ireland and was used by the Church to spread Christianity throughout the land. Similarly to convert the remaining Celts the symbol was used as a reminder of casting out Satan like the snakes. Whilst the witches of Ireland, rejected Christianity with their own celebration on the Saints feast day, continued in their own Satanic practices.

It was hard not to get caught up in the hurly-burly of Tom's indoctrination. Our conversation was stopped abruptly as the weather had turned fowl and the wind and rain forced us both back to the broad walk. I said my goodbyes to the good humoured Irishman and made my journey back to the comfort of my room. I was up bright and early the next morning as the sun came up through the rain and was pleased to see sunshine although the day turned to bitter coldness. I walked the city of Galway and made my way to the dock lands to board an early ferry for the Aran Islands. My port of call where I had booked accommodation was Inishmore which I soon found was the tourist haven for the three of the Aran islands. The ferry arrived to the historic village at the waterfront amid an armada of people coming in from elsewhere on other ferries. I proceeded to make my way to a cafe for coffee before walking for around thirty minutes along a coastal road to the "Tigh Fitz' guesthouse for a two nights stay.

The next morning I walked most of the East coast and across a meadow and all to view the west coast and island from the opposite shore, Apart from stopping at a pub on the West side for a drink and hot chips, I walked all day to explore this ancient place. I resolved to hire a bike the next day to explore more of the west coast that was more wild and rugged than the East. So the next day, I was up again bright and early, returning to the village and at the waterfront hired a bike for the day. It proved to be a wise move and I rode around the coastline taking in the historic sights and sat down near a beach watching a large seal floating on its back asleep on a flat sea taking in the warmth of the sun. The whole island I observed as one big rock farm, as it was when Irish whalers settled in the late 1800s, intent on harpooning whales for oil to cook their fish and provide light for their humble abode. This historical hunters and gatherers turned to farming and crop growing had to climb down steep cliff faces to gather what soil they could embedded between rocks blown by the winds from the mainland.

The women initially gathering seaweed in baskets whilst the men continued to hunt for whales. A combined effort of the early Irish inhabitants worked to hammer and break down rocks of which they created furrowed mounds. The seaweed was dumped with the gathered soil and over time they cleared, gardened and planted potatoes and other vegetables from seeds obtained on the mainland. Over time cleared areas and soil beds produced grasses and the subsistence farmers introduced livestock. Today this is quite a large area of meadow, crops and cattle to be seen but even more rocks are present on what may still be called rock farming. The whalers and hardy farmers were still doing this back-breaking work and primitive fishing methods right up to the early 1930s. I noted that possibly the greenest area on the whole Island was the local golf course that proudly displays the American flag. It belongs to Donald Trump!

It rained on my return ferry journey back to mainland Galway and it rained and rained for my remaining time in Ireland. I walked wet and ridden with a flu virus long before I finely gave up for a return to Australia and my own bed to recover. I had visited the Spanish wall, noting the connection of the fishermen who built it with the Irish fishermen who had made their way to Finisterre. The Irish who had travelled to the end of the earth in Spain to fish had introduced the Uilleann pipes to the Spanish and to this day have over sixty percent of their blood DNA that of Spanish origin, so they did more than fish there. Not to be outdone, I left Galway and made my way on the Burren Way, despite feeling like death warmed up. Another week of walking in wet clothing, uphill and down dale, nature had finally beaten me, I was exhausted. It was time to go home as the rash on my skin that I had under control after my 2013 Camino had flared up again and my body ached with pain, not so much from the physical effort I had put myself through but more that I was physically ill. I did not finish the Burren Way walk and have no desire to finish it in the future either. In less than six weeks I had walked near 1200 kilometres and had experienced every, physical, mental and spiritual emotion that could be imagined on my journeys of my 2017 Camino, Wicklow Mountains, Aran Island and Burren Way. To the rest of Ireland, the land of my ancestors on both sides of my family tree, it would have to wait for some future date if ever in this lifetime. The rain still fell ever so gently on my soul as I winged my way back home via Dublin and Paris and back to Australia, my homeland, the land of the free.

The months that followed saw me examining my reason for living and hoping as I recovered from my ordeal. Sometimes in dreams I was visited by the old Major General Count Cherep-Spiridovick who pricked my consciousness on spiritual reality and retold me of the foundation stones of a One World Order mission and the banking system that was to follow. The system of credit that became a reality, as mankind reached out for more to sustainability wants over needs. The endless pursuits of ideas and actions that cost much resulting in both good and equally not so. At other times Jesus appeared to me with his own set of instructions for a better way to live, if I but took up his mantle. Then at other times, I was left alone to be free to do as I please and not be bothered by consequence. Sometimes my mind floated back to the years of my childhood, catching fish and killing lizards for the fun of it or duck shooting with a shot gun. The thought of cleaning the duck for a family feast or climbing a tree to take a bird's egg from a nest, clearing its content by pin pricking both ends and blowing it out with my mouth, placing the shell with all my other coloured collection into a sawdust bed and hiding the treasure in an old shoe box for later viewing. Sometimes just watching my growing silk worm collection turn from moth to butterfly and at other times I was not content until I found a quiet river or beach to walk nearby to contemplate my navel, consider past misgivings and seek a way forward.

My boyhood dreams came to me as did the voices of my own children and grandchildren and all too soon they fade away again and I was left alone in the silent darkness. Sometimes when in vacant mood I would catch myself dreaming of a youth long gone, of dreams that were once important to me and are of little consequence now. Memories of the clop, clop of the baker's cart as the daily bread for the family was delivered and the milkman with bottles rattling in a crate full of milk came by, filling our larder with fresh milk topped with cream. The green grocer knocking at the door with his locally grown fruit and vegetables to top up family supplies or the medicine men, like the Rowley's traveler with his miracle cures of natural remedies for illness also came. Such memories come and go as I grow older and look back on what seems a distant past. They were the good old days, growing up in a timber town, where a man could earn a good living cutting timber, growing bananas or fruit for transport to the city markets. Where the butcher cured and sold his own meat and where a man could get a job or be entrepreneurial and build his own empire with little capital outlay. When a wife was content to stay at home and looked after house and a brood of growing kids. A time when fishermen sold their catch on Friday because it was the traditional day to eat fish.

Those were the good times when people cared for their fellow man's welfare as much as their own. The foundation stones of my local Mid North Coast community of a quiet little timber town evolved from Irish immigrants, who made their way north from city life for timber work, cutting sleepers to connect the Sydney to Brisbane north coast train. Initially the timber getters cross cut sawed trees dropping them to the forest floor, chopped by hand and smoothed with tools, then dragged the felled tree by bullock dray to the rail side for foundation sleepers for the rail train. Fettler's, who later lived in tents by the track building the train line, lived on meagre pay and depended on passing trains for a supply of smokes, booze and current news from the big smoke, Sydney. Communities grew up around the timber mills that followed the track along the North Coast. These were later followed by immigrants from Europe and Asia. Following the 20th century World Wars, they grew in number, many arrived from Italy and established themselves in the banana growing industry, fruit and vegetables, whilst others created dairy farms and still others a small goods factory. Like most north coast townships mine grew other industries, but the population of my boyhood were predominantly of Irish descent. By the time I had reached my teens a growing timber industry thrived as did milk production, beef exports , banana growing and fruit and vegetables supplying to the cities. Exports supported by road transport sea and rail linked the township growing into a thriving community; boasting hotels, motels, a district hospital, swimming pool, golf course, showground for sporting events, entertainment venues and churches of every denomination. It was the way townships grew in those days, initially from the back of those immigrants born in Ireland.

My mind at its darkest relived more of the pending plans of those men of a secret society of One World Order. In my days of born illnesses I devoted much time to research and now considered in my head a vision of the future. I saw the world's countries in my min's eye as if they were represents by animals of all types as their symbol. I did not see then that I would be influenced by my creative muse to write a book on One World Government and songs of my own making.

Now listen very carefully
you will get it in the drift,
it's all within the music
and any chorus riff !

We are the music makers,
we are the tellers of dreams
shattering the sounds of silence,
at least that's how it seems.

Our quest moves to a beat,
you must stay in tune
listen to the lyrics,
as we cry out to the moon !

Take the journey inward
the ancient way within,
you may catch it if you listen,
it's in a chorus riff din !

We are the Atlas Eaters,
a voice for the dreamers of dreams
within world lost and forsaken,
singing its death knell it seems.

We master the words of the dreamer
helped by The Master it seems,
tune makers of the trampled,
guides to our youthful dreams !

We are the music makers
the teller of tales so it seems,
we've music to play, words for today,
nations are animal themes.

"The Lion roars in the jungle,
  the Bear's free to roam about,
  whilst The Herd looks on
  to the King of Beast for truth."

The King has lost his crown
for the herd is at loss
whilst The King just sits
pawing at the ground.

The Kiwi is travelling with the sheep,
the Kangaroos keeping up pace,
Elephants long on the memory,
The Owl has a scowl on his face !

The Lion and the pride search the sky,
trusting the past may return,
hoping against all reason,
The Eagle will once more soar.

Watching for signs of the changing,
when the animals all gather as one,
some will be held in cages,
whilst The Bear is angry and proud !

And the rest with some fear
search the sky now,
whilst The Eagle is is soaring about
and The Dragon keeps wearing the crown !

Now if you listen carefully,
you will get it in the drift,
it's within all our music
and any chorus riff !

We are the prophets of truth
we are the prophet of doom,
take note of the lyrics
it's all in the animals tune.

There was once a crab apple tree that in the winter of my discontent
lost its leaves as deciduous trees do. It sat in a garden surrounded by
a most beautiful array of delicate evergreens and perennials awaiting
the springtime to flower, as such of what nature does. The garden of
this Eden was attended by a devout gardener, an angel of great horti-
cultural talent whose living spirit was embedded in the planting, sowing and keeping of the joy of nature's creation. To protect the environment that surrounds the work of art the gardener planted a hedge of
green that grew to be a boundary and a labyrinth to wander a puzzle
of complexity as it drew one to contemplation. So the sower did plant
and nurture in order that, we who suffer the slings and arrows of out-
rageous fortune might retreat too and reap the rewards of the angel's

most diligent efforts. I know not what drew the angel to such every changing natural task, because at heart this one was an artist of great renown. However, it seems she got more reward from the changing seasons and the landscape garden than the still life of painting of a bowl of flowers or the brush of carefree strokes of a bush scene that she quite easily could so create.

Now I knew nothing of the names of the trees she attended too, nor the plants and flowers she had sown; not their Latin nor common known ones. Then my only attraction, save for the angel who attended the garden was that crab apple tree's comfort to my miserable soul at the time. The winter that came down upon me then was of a particularly dark and cold one and nature had reserved such an event as it was solely for me. It was there in that garden that I somehow resonated with that crab apple tree, for it stood without leaves, standing awkward, raw and skeleton like in its nakedness. I had felt desolate and exposed to the elements like that crab apple. It was in those times of cloudy thoughts and lonely feelings that I sought out the crab apple tree to gaze upon its craggy outer skin and lifelessness. It is then that I had taken heart from the crab apple, even though it appeared raw and awkward in its nakedness, standing alone there in a garden of green. Its shear audacity to stand naked and spindly, whilst the rest of nature that surrounded it was alive and vibrant despite the winter chill in the air. The crab apple seemed as if it was waiting for spring change to come again, already with small buds appearing on its branches giving a hint of spring to follow, despite its cold empty aloofness. I must say I cannot remember what the crab apple flowers look like and in the past didn't really care. However, in that winter of my own fragility, irritability and discontent, I had looked forward to the coming spring. The hour is always darkest before the dawn and I knew, with patience, despite my then circumstance, like the crab apple, I would bloom again in the spring.

Looking beyond the garden into some distant past, I could see a small boy running through the bush with his friends of a very young age. Our playground was always the bush in the spring and early summer until it got too hot and too dangerous to play there and then it was off to the beach. We were granted great insight into nature by our own experience and what we didn't know we looked up in the Encyclopaedia. Our common ground with palms, flannel flower, yellow tail flower, brown pea, spider orchids, warpath, honeysuckle and Christmas bells was all in a day's exploration! In our days of hunting, killing lizards by hand with just a knife, avoiding snakes and climbing trees for eggs and searching the ground to get yet another for our collection. The colours and variety was enormous for the keen eyes of young boys and we ardently collected from species to species. The ground nesting birds nests were well camouflaged to avoid predators like us, snakes and lizards, especially the blue tongue lizards.

In climbing trees we were more likely to be attacked by the Magpie who protected their nest eggs from us gathering any eggs. Using their beaks like a knife to attack the heads of young boy's intent on robbery was always a challenge. The prize of collecting a pale blue egg with its olive brown markings, signified each of us as a warrior amongst our peers. Nothing however match the number and variety of eggs we had in our collection and always the variety of the same species, like the ocean blue of the black tit to the green blue of the great tit with its bone markings. There was never more than one or two of us in our hunting parties and we had a code, no more than one egg from a nest, thus leaving the mother to tend to her remainder for hatching. Even then, built into our nature was some semblance of the environmentalist.

Of course, we had an equal code for our ability to kill something of God's nature to prove how skilled and superior we were to our mates. Making a shanghai which classically consisted of a strong y-shaped frame cut from a fork in a tree and strung with two rubber strips cut from old tyre tubes usually found at the back of the shed at home or the tyre service bay in town. The rubber strips led back to a pocket, often taken from the leather upper of a worn out shoe, and that held the stone projectile. The dominant hand grabbed the pocket and drew it back to the desired extent of power for the projectile; sufficient enough to kill any bird high in a tree with one aim and fire off the weapon. I used to have to hide my shanghai under the back staircase at home or with my birds nest collection in a shoe box in dad's car garage. My father did not permit me to have anything that interfered with the natural flow of nature and I always had to hide what I was doing in that regard. My mother, on the other hand didn't object too much and this helped me justify my collection and my improved skills in a kill with my then chosen weapon. I had a true aim, having honed it with help from my Uncle Fred who loaded my first shot out of a .303 bolt action when I was only five. He taught me how to aim, breath steady, hold my breath at the appropriate moment then pull the trigger. I downed my first Magpie on my first shot and got a pat on the back for the effort. I wonder now if those returned soldiers, with the thought of World War 11 just ended could justify teaching children to shoot. I guess they considered learning to shoot was a skill worth mastering in the event of a future world war when a call to arms might be inflicted upon my generation too.

In my later married years I graduated to owning a gun shop for a time and It was quite lucrative for me too. Particularly as apart from guns I sold a great variety of ammunition and the police back then were more open to a person having a licence to use a firearm. My proprietorship of the world of guns ceased when one of my customers blew his brains out with a shotgun just two weeks after purchasing one from me. It was later revealed that he owned lots of shotguns so it was unlikely that he particularly chose the gun I had sold him to kill himself. His son confirmed this and advised me not to worry so much but It was enough for me to sell my gun supplies to a good friend who was more inclined to use them for kangaroo culling. So that took the pressure off and I handed in my right to sell guns to the local police and walked away. I have had no desire to pick up a gun since let alone kill anything. A local purchased the right to sell guns and set up a gun shop in town a few weeks after I closed mine down. He shot himself within the year at his shop after losing a great deal of money one weekend gambling. It has been common practice for many years now for bush men to kill themselves this way and often take family members with them. The number has grown over recent years in Australia, particularly with the ever increasing blight of mental illness due to depression, anxiety and stressful economic circumstance, growing debt and banking pressures to repay debt. There was a time you could see your way clear with a bank to buy a considerable amount of time to ride out financial difficulties but those days are long gone, as avarice has overruled compassion.

Nature's law eventually brought me back to my senses with the closure of my gun business, as did my passion to climb the corporate tree. That too ended in disaster but not so much that I wasn't successful. I was. It was my excessive drinking and extreme enthusiasm to get things done at the expense of my health. In a sense I ran my race against all natural cause and the ultimate was full blown alcoholism, depression, anxiety, mental and physical exhaustion that eventually took its toll and landed me more than once into rehabilitation. I thought I could make my way back through relationships, new business ventures and rekindle my enthusiasm for living on the edge, but when I crashed for the last time in all those areas of my life, I ultimately returned to nature to recover. This resulted in my spending hours walking the beaches and mountain tracks both at home and overseas and a realisation that nature and my fellowman played more of a part to my recovery than my own introspection. Thinking back now to the devout gardener, the angel of the garden where once there was a crab apple tree, I mused a little over the fact that I had resonated so much with that tree, the angel and the garden when at my natural lowest. Upon recovery I returned to the garden and found that it had all been altered considerably since my last visit. The gardener had long since moved on and like me had taken a new directional change for her betterment. On investigation the crab apple tree had not flowered as it had done in previous years in spring and had died. It was eventually uprooted, its seeds, branches and dead leaves mulched and spread into the soil for a new garden. The crab apple had been there for me in all of its nakedness to serve a purpose at that time, as I suppose had the gardener. Now for my life there is a far different kind of gardener; a new way to flourish in what might be called a God given nature.

CHAPTER 6.

THE NATURE OF THINGS

The icicles pierced like needles on my cheeks, hands and the part of my ears that protruded beyond my balaclava head protection, as I tramped every weary step towards the top of the mountain peak. Visibility was not good but better than I expected under the circumstances. The eye goggles were saving me from snow blindness and I thanked the almighty for that. A pause to check myself over and my equipment before I endeavoured to take a further step forward on the narrow precipice. Mountaineering waterproof boots, crampons for the vertical points of the peak ahead, ice axe in a sheet over my shoulder were all secure. Pulling the pants and jacket cords tighter so as not to allow any wind in, I checked the rest of my gear then. Climbing ropes, climbing harness, belay, rapper extension, two curved ice climbing tools, trekking poles all secure. I had two litres of spare drinking water in my back pack and ample snow and ice around me so I had no fear of dehydration. As for solids, a tasty variety of high energy bars would see me through until I returned to base camp. I had figured that if I got stuck up there in a blizzard or snow drift, I had enough woollen underwear and socks to see me through until the weather turned back to bearable conditions. The fleece shirt, jacket and waterproof pants all added to my sense of security in not being frozen to death, but the conditions up there were hazardous. I found myself praying for some relief from the short breaths I needed to take in order to beat altitude sickness. Every step I climbed was deliberately placed with the angle of the foot and the body given a quick calculation as to grip on the ice rock surface, consciously aware of the risk of falling into the abyss.

Equally my left hand gripped the protruding stone edges of the mountain rock wall whilst at the same time my right hand held the stock to help keep balance. It was a precarious predicament in which I found myself hanging to a ledge in blizzard conditions almost blind from the snow drift, lost to the sound of a howling wind, upon a mountain track some 6500 metres above sea level. There was no room for error, no lapse of concentration, nothing there but the mastering of fear overcome with the energy of pure adrenalin pumping through my veins. I was conscious of time slowing within a void of nothingness, nothing there except for me and the mountain. Time then seemed to slow down as my sense of perception heightened and all the colours of the rainbow appeared before me, as the wind slowed, the icicles ceased to penetrate my face and colours appeared sharper and brighter than whatever I had witnessed before and whatever sound drifted to this great height seemed to ripple into my mind's eye and out again to the vision that so suddenly appeared before me. One minute there was nothing but white, the next a majestic visa of pure beauty of sun reflection on coloured rocks and sheer peaks above and below me for a far as the eye could see. There was welling up within me a sense of aliveness, connectedness to the mountain and the infinite world that surrounded me on that razor edge where I stood. I was moving a little faster having rested, moving with precision and poise to the very pinnacle of this great mountain vista. The feeling of touching the void within and without slowly subsided as the sign of aliveness and peace I had just experienced slowly receded and all too quickly faded into memory, filed away for some instant recall in some future appropriate time. As I made my way down the mountain, I could not wait to experience the sheer exhilaration again and I was already planning in my head another climb. I wanted to experience that complete letting go, in mind, in body and in spirit. None who hasn't climbed a mountain can understand or experience mindfulness a mountain climb does to one. To be caught up in the mountain and that state of vibrant awareness, connectedness and peace is so much in the mind more than the actual reality of the event.

I guess without having experienced that journey to the top of the mountain I could not have believed before the climb that I don't really need a mountain to find that blissful feeling again in this lifetime. I have done it the hard way, got fit for the distance and the esteem of the event but reality now told, I need not go through the rigours of extreme pain and exhaustion to make the fitness level to be able to do such a climb again. My age had me now reflect on the reality that it was highly unlikely that I could make such a journey to the top of such a mountain a second time. I had the presence of mind to realise that if I we willing to do some self-exploration and let go everything that weighted down my body and mind then a deep and lofty place could be experienced without ever setting foot on a mountain trail again. I could be being prepared now, to welcome the infinite expansion of a happy feeling, of an empty mind and a universe of knowingness, of experiencing the divine and the grace of bliss. It was as simple as emptying oneself, of being present in the now, of not holding on to anything nor anybody. Sitting in a chair I could breathe that state of mind as easy as I could sweep with a broom. It was all just a matter of perception, of accepting me as I am in the present, letting go my addiction to suffering that I had been so traditionally conditioned to. Holding the key to happiness was not the thing either. It was more about living happy irrespective of actions, events, other people or things in the outer world beyond me.

The great secret to my happiness was and has always been within me not the world. The most difficult part was learning to relax and rest, taking heart in the simplicity of life, finding balance and equanimity of my mind. Once all the worries of the world were put aside and negativity and fear released, then and only then could I know peace. Living in a relaxed state of mind did not come easy for me as a multitasking energetic doer. A voice inside my head repeated 'learn to be not to do.' It was a hard lesson that had to be practiced. Just to go with the flow, to be not to do in frantic actions based on the endless pursuit of ideas. It was coming to me slowly but surely to not only quiet my mind and listen to the sweet silence within my spirit but to listen to my body. A body that was worn down by so much physical activity that it ached for release. Even my skin, if I listen to it was saying 'hush, be still." It had taken a long hard road of much suffering, loss of love and life that had bought me to this place. I had tried to relive such inner turmoil of mind, body and spirit through over indulging in everything from eating to sex, to work, from spiralling highs to disposing lows. There had been no rest for me being used to living on limited sleep and too busy to slow down and smell the roses. Now it was different, for I had time to stop, listen and learn from that still small voice inside, telling me gently that it was not all about me. I realised then it was about him, the God of my nature for him and for me ultimately culminating in love for my fellow man. I was stepping back now from inner negative thinking to a positive well-being. I had given up the struggle to be what was expected of me by others and began too focused on a choice of bliss in whatever comes my way. He would lead me, would show me the way that was to be my lot for the remainder of my life. I had the free will to do as I pleased but my best thinking an egotistical nature had eventually put me in a rehab; more than once and I was not going back there.

I had walked The Way of St. James on the Camino three times, climbed every mountain that had been placed in my path, fell in and out of love more times than I care to remember, tried it all, drugs, sex and rock n roll. Many moments and hours I had given as a listening ear to others who sought my good counsel or those who just wanted to dump on me. I had been used for my leadership qualities, my ability to make money, my friendship and what had appeared as kindness and all had come to nothing, lost and broken as I was. Then came the unkindest cut of all, I had been used by my family. Those that blamed me for the suicide of my son when it had nothing to do with my attitude and actions but to be a loving father who was in his alcoholic ways trying to teach a wayward son how to overcome his troubled mind. His death, like so many other tragedies that surrounded me back then had almost killed me. In point of fact I had longed for death back then. Now though, I was doing my best to let go my past and my ego, driven now by my God given creative talents to do whatever and whichever my God's leading me too for the greater good of all concerned. So it was in the empty void of consciousness on the mountain peaks and on the plateau I emptied my inner plans, fear and worries. My inner beings then was for a time content just to be. Then, just when I thought I had it, the answer to it all, some random idea springs to life, to reform something and I was away again.

The realisation that I have not got the golden thread as I had perceived in the silence of an emptied mind. The stillness helped, the silence added new dimension, as did the new neural pathways in my brain. But I all too quickly reverted to my previous state of restlessness and self- seeking. It would take more practice, more disciplined time to meditate into nothingness, continuing to be in the present in the now in real time. I resolved not to jump to every idea with an action deemed necessary at a precise time. Just continue to be and do as things come up, to be planned but for the now with a written guide but not an agenda as such. Much like making a grocery list that one puts together before going shopping so as not to forget what is required in the act of doing.

So a continued listening to the body, the mind the spirit in sequence, in meditative state seemed to me for now to be the key to my being. A quote from W. Somerset Maugham came to me, "it's a long arduous road he's starting to travel, but it may be that at the end of it he will find what he is seeking." I smiled to myself at the thought of what makes my mind go around, the random thoughts that drove me here and there. To do what I need to do and at the same time live in a perfect state of ease and comfort, it would not only take time and patience, it would require money for food, clothing and shelter, to achieve such a delicate plan. Another W. Somerset Maugham quote came to mind which made me smile again at the thought of it: "Money is like a sixth sense without which you cannot make complete use of the other five." Yes, I had always used money as my measurement method for my success, but it no longer ruled me.

The goal I knew was to make the best of the unanswered in the beat of the heart of my universe, to pit nature with nature. To see the path laid out before me, I need to stop and evaluate it and make some sense to go that way. To realise one path that opens up may not become my path for the future unless I choose it to be so, despite my natural instincts telling me otherwise. I had ultimately to take all future steps as I had taken past ones that proved in the long run to be the wrong ones but without which I would not have learnt necessary lessons for living now. My own path I now chose to make with deliberation every step I take now is my own, chosen by me and none other. I choose my luck as I chose my steps, for it is my way, not the way of some long forgotten saint, some hero of a past; a thing that was done by them that made them what they were, this being my time now. I was no saint, no military hero, just plain old natural me, doing the best that I can with the talents I now use to go ever onward. These talents that I have been given to use as best I can in the service of my fellowman and ultimately I trust in my God's service too.

There are new beginnings being extended to use every day. A God calling within our own circumstance, to move forward into life. An opportunity to explore new possibilities into which we are invited so that our hearts might not lose sight of freshness in our coming of age, our hearts are always being drawn towards the sacred within but we so often are distracted by the false premise of what it is that we so earnestly seek. There is a magic in every beginning wrote the German philosopher Herman Hesse. No truer statement can be had that this as in the birth of a child, the growth and delight of the purity of childhood. A creative idea brought to life and lived may expand into an equally delightful feeling as it grows and matures into a nature of its own. We observe our child grow ever so quickly, caught between the immediate experience of the present and the heightened expectation of the future- a fulfilled moment in the dawning of a new day.

So another German writer noted: 'Childhood and youth are transfigured with the daybreak colours of the dawn of life, of imagine childhood innocence, the image of pure beginning and unlimited possibilities- all this makes childhood the image of hope and who we search for- 'the child in us. It is because we long to open this wellspring in our selves once more.' It is the challenge to recover that child and the challenge in our ageing years that we might blow away the chaff of many things, so as to reveal the essential wheat of our remaining time on earth. "Our souls are always young. They have preserved, in a safe place, the fields of dreams that once lay beautifully across the landscapes of our childhood. It is these fields, and in no other, where the seeds of our God-like beauty were first nurtured that our eternal harvest will be reaped. We do not outgrow our childhood. We grow into it more fully as we grow older. And it is only in heaven that we will possess it completely." So said Daniel O' Leary in a recent article I had read.

Every child represents a new beginning in life …original, completely incomparable and in every way strengthening, confirming great hope for the victory of life that each of us cherish deep within us even in the midst of distortions on our lives journeys- our failures, our cynicism and frustrations. The divine has set before us to become as a child, to be reborn as it were, no matter our circumstance, we can begin again and become refreshed. The call to die unto self that I might live, be released of the blockages of my defects of character and be renewed to the natural spirit of that which is God given. To break open the tomb that I could then see beyond the limited blockages of imaginative fear. The creative flame rekindled, I began to breathe again, weep again, laugh again, love again. The child within, ever opened to the dawning of fullness of life, born again to stretch out into the future once more. The river of the waters of the one that could be heard crying in the desert; John the Baptist who had administered the waters off the Jordan, baptising Jesus in the cleansing unto the Father, the eternal Godhead has been carried throughout the ages as upon me. So the gift of creative renewal and insight I felt and was free in my meditative state to act once more for my own good and the good of all concerned.

The real artist within works with complete absorption and utter concentration upon a sand- painting which must be destroyed as the sun sets and the tide comes in. He knows his work, as concrete product, will vanish within a single day but the healing that it has accomplished will live again, a re- creation, and all who have participated in this ceremony will have shared in the creation and rebirth of power. Here the creative power works not through original creation, but through exact and patterned imitation, a meticulous obedience to ordained ritual, and the image which is held in the contemplation of the worshipper works potently within him. Here obedience is not repression but dedication and control, not being in opposition to but in the service of creativity.The sand- painter's personal achievement is swallowed up in identification with the healing power of the God. He transmits power through obedience. The measure of the healing is proportionate to the spiritual participation of those who take part, either actively or through receptivity as witness of the event of creativity or just as an absorber, soaking up the energy spiritually within themselves or in unison with others. In all such experiences the whole being is in a state of heightened receptivity, of intuitive awareness and desire. For creative energy must submit to discipline and hard work, but its source is desire. The Creator's sand painting may wash away with the tide but the desire lives on in paradise.

Turning my head to the heavens, I watched the reflection of the sinking sun on the space station and wondered what the sixteen nations who participate in the 'programme and research' that is continually taking place up there have in mind for the 'metal star, ' As for us below, a Nuclear Armageddon transpires here on earth. With U.S. oil sanctions on Iran and Russia and taxes imposed on China supply to U.S markets and Nuclear rockets ready to be launched at the flick off a switch, one wonders what the game plan is for the next faze of the current super powers. I was pondering the sanity of navy war games with the U.S, Australia and Japan actions in our waters with Chinas 'spy' ship watching on nearby and recent allowance of two of China's war ships to sit quietly in our Harbour. It is no small wonder why the youth of the day just live for the moment in a frenzied fear of what's going on. Lyrical words from a sonf of of Four Blondes whispered:

"And so I wake in the morning
And I step outside
and I take a deep breath and I get real high
And I scream from the top of my lungs
What's going on? What going on? "

CHAPTER 7.

CLEAR AND PRESENT DANGER

There is a tear in my eye as I write these lines, seeing the world I have known coming to an end and a clear reality of my journey thus far that has not contributed much to the benefit of my fellow man. Sure I achieved apparent success in the world of consumerism, financial freedom and institutional belief in a job well done. I had married and had a family and was a good provider as I was meant to be, but all that way of life crumbled as I forgot the Golden rule in favour of the alternate route that I came to accept as the norm of the world of the hand in the dark. In the end my way of life led me only to darkness, despair, regret and a thirst for another drink. Ultimately change does happen and sanity prevailed and I am back in the land of the living with a clarity of vision that I never saw in my ever blind pursuits of ideas and action in my former life. I am an old man now and a little worn and constantly weary but I have courage and determination and the will to win is still rumbling beneath the surface. Now my life is quite a different story, for it's more of a 'Let go and Let God' approach to all I see and do. I reason that I am just a vessel in the hand of the God of my own understanding and not the hand in the dark that I was a pawn to for most of my former life, but now I have sight and a vision for the future.

We are living in a time when we are unwittingly being pushed to the edge. We are slowly but surely losing faith in the institutions that previously formed the structures of our lives that we lived by. We struggle to look with admiration and respect to our governments, judiciary, politicians, religious, educational systems, churches or economy. The society we have known is crumbling and we have raped and pillaged Mother Earth and she like us is trying to find her balance. Mother nature she can't cope.

We must make a new start and that means we must act within the bounds of confidentiality in all we see and do in-order to make real inroads into progressiveness. Healing change doesn't start with the collective view, it starts with the individual not taking sides, not speaking out but being more of a passive listener. We need to relearn how to allow ones personal viewpoint to be heard above another and only speaking one at a time in a group. We may think we hear and know but we have lost that ability to take on board what is being said for our individual and collective benefit. To use our powers of discernment for the good of all concerned is a very powerful thing, so we must really hear what is being said rather than react to what is said. If a person or collective group feels miserable, depressed, suicidal, peaceful, positive or negative, it is not our place to tell them how they should or should not feel. If that's the individual or collective feeling then it is what it is. The key to progress is to let things settle and the solution will come up to solve the situation. We don't need an adviser, pills, or bombs to be dropped to resolve anything.

We are living in ever present danger of nuclear war in a faster and still faster world of change, in a progressive realisation of new life habits in food consumption, new ways of dress and means of communication, in a world of work and play. Our modern world gives scant regard to individual freedom in favour of brainwashing of the masses into living and breathing what has been pre-programmed and planned for the future of mankind and our planet. Man has lost the ability to reason in favour of acceptance of self- satisfaction of our brainwashed reality as we are lulled into a false sense of security and wellbeing that in reality is untrue. It is time to wake up and see what lies underneath the sur-face of you and me as our God given directive and not what is the plan of evil over good. I cannot say what is the truth for you as I dare not breathe what is the truth for me. It is for each of us to remove the scales from our eyes that we might see and in seeing we shall believe and act on that belief as we are supposed to do and are destined to do. Until we face that reality we are doomed to what awaits us orches-trated by the ever present hand in the dark. Armageddon is on our door step and we have much to be afraid of for our personal and col-lective security, for the worst outcomes clearly awaits us on many fronts if we are not vigilant now.

It may come in the form of a Nuclear World War or an earth shattering economic collapse, another mutation of an out of control Covid like flu virus or unexpected lack of supply of our bare necessities. It may mu-tate into riots in the streets, global internet failure or a currency col-lapse or lack of fuel to keep the first world economies afloat, but mark my words, it will come and there are signs everywhere you look on the planet, for it may be closer than you think. The Armageddon will pass in a shorter time span than has been predicted by soothsayers and for that matter biblical predictions, but many millions could die as a con-sequence. Prayer may help starve off the worst of it and charity of both individual and collective nature to those less fortunate will cer-tainly help, but charity alone will not completely solve the problems that beset us in this old world. However there is a ray of great hope and it is not with those of us in the afternoon of our lives, nor those that sweat and strain in the heat of the noon day sun, nor those who are in the morning of their lives, but it is with the children of the future, those who are at the dawning, those just near to and reaching the age of reason, our children's' children. To them collective history and the lesson there need not go back beyond the 20th century to see the havoc, mass murder and devastation inflicted on humanity from two world wars, the killing fields of Pol Pot in Cambodia, the napalm bombings of villages in Vietnam, the pathways of assassinations that beset every decade of that century for the cause of peace, and prosperity of our first world nations. It's the poverty of spirit, mind and body that decimates the worlds of rich and poor alike.

These first two decades of this 21st century show we have just as much contempt for humanity as we did in the previous one. Already this century we continue with much bloodshed, depression, suicide, and an ever growing flood of mental disorder brought on by our lifestyle, greed and lust for power as well as continued international poverty in third world countries. The Earth itself rejected our folly resulting in earthquakes, flood, fire and famine. These first two decades of the 21st century has been no better than the folly of our last one and we are still going about our businesses like all is normality, but deep down we know that it isn't. The little children of the future may look back with much wisdom on what has been done that cast a shadow over our world in the recent history of their parents and grandparents. However, the Armageddon or whatever transpires that will cause massive change will be in their primary years and they are already showing signs of greatness in endeavours that are beyond our wildest imagination. They are already using the parts of their mental capacity that is far beyond the 10% of brain power that we have used throughout our lifetime. These children of a great age will do works, word and deeds of unimaginable beauty and progression in their natural state. We, the parents and grandparents of the now, to a great degree will have laid the foundations of a 21st century brave new world for them despite our erroneous ways.

The advances of mobile phones to digital wrist watches are taken for granted by present generations. Ultimately a DNA coded personal algorithmically programmed number will be inserted underneath the skin of the   future advanced generation of children. The clothing we purchase today in all its variety of size, shapes, colours and forms shall be replaced with a graphene substance which will model to the shape of the human body of the wearer changing in colour and temperature according to the feelings and mood of the individual. Genetically modified food will be the order of the day, with flavours, colour and shapes to match the feelings and personality of the consumer. Consumption of these 'products' will sustain life and include necessary chemicals to ward-off any potential infection or disease. DNA of the newborn will be engineered and modified according to the needs of those who control choice. Choice will be programmed giving just enough feeling to make all thought appear to be free. A central controlled information stream will administer, control and record every thought, word and deed of the individual. Autonomous self-propelling driverless vehicles will rocket across the skies on invisible grid patterns as well as on the ground and on land masses developed on and beneath the ocean, taking passengers to their central work locations for their appointed time of working on digital screens linked to a mainframe computer in a space station. Everything will be mapped out and there will be no more need of individual goals, religious myths to believe in, nor the tight bonds of history, for all that will be erased in this brave new world of our children's children life on this planet. All that we have known from our history, from our past will be erased in favour of a single computer system that records everything and it is now, in this current world for the powers that be are jockeying for position for a final show down of who controls what at the appointed time when the hand in the dark will come, and his majestic number embedded in his forehead, which may be interpreted as 666, shall take his place at the Temple in the City of God, high on the mountain top and the world will change forever. This may well be a none to subtle interpretation of the Book of Revelations, but if it be true then the man who bears the number 666 will rain for a time bringing more death, distraction, destruction, disease and pestilence in biblical proportions to our world. His mission is already in play in our world of gluttonous using up of our precious earthly resources and those of our own thought in our person folly.

The weapons of mass destruction are in position by those who seek to continue to control everything and the trigger is poised waiting to be pulled. It may be a nuclear bomb, the release of a laboratory manufactured disease with known human death consequences or it may be as simple as the flick of a switch to disconnect the world of communication by the members of the Hand in the Dark from the far off Space Shuttle. We do not know the time nor the appointed hour and it must be clear that we must ready ourselves to walk a new path for the sake of future generations if the world is to survive.

After the Armageddon, if you have not thought about God and his message built into us individually, it will be too late to do so. The new pathway of light, of lessons of peace and simple techniques for our survival will be taught by the hand that rocks the cradle. It is a time for us to be aware, to be as vigilant as a female serpent and as gentle as a dove, to love our personal concept of God above as we see fit to listen to the small still voice within. We may not hear it on our first listening as we run headlong through life like a blizzard, thinking that we are the wizards of desire and destiny. We may not even hear it as we have the wisdom to meditate or hear the music that soothes the savage beast within us all. But we will ultimately hear it if we go to the silence of our soul, to scan the body, the mind and our spirit. We have the freedom now to do this, to listen to what exactly is going on within and hear the message of what we must act upon for the future of the young. It is there in our cave of self- awareness that we will find him of which we seek, of peace of understanding of clarity of thinking and reasoning. It is there that we have the realisation that we are not in control of ourselves or our destiny, but that we have the free will to choose over erroneous thoughts and actions in favour of that which is of the God of our own understanding within our human spirit. For at the appointed time we are the catalyst to the brave new world of the future generations.We are the ones who can teach the young of the errors of our way. We are the ones who can choose the path to darkness or the path to light from the depth of our souls, laying down beneficial foundations for those of our children children's children. In our lifetime of the 20th century and 21st centuries we have advanced science, medical knowledge, methods of food production, advancement in mechanical technology, computerisation, means of communication, education, world explorations into the unknown on earth, under the sea and in space. Equally we have advanced our own destructive nature with a way of life that has alarming increases in suicide amongst the young, out of control drug taking bringing many to an early grave, mental disorder and lack of faith, warped value systems and a sense of hopelessness. We must act with our experience and talents to advance the course of our humanity. It's a must for those of our age to keep on trying for our link to the heart and soul for the future little ones and the survival of our planet.

I was in deep contemplation, seated on a rocky cliff face looking out across the mountains of the Pyrenees into the great beyond and considering those things of the known knowns and the known unknowns. Gazing now at the valley floor below and thinking of the past that was and the future of humanity of the living now and the dead now gone. My mind was back in that grave yard of my son for a moment, it was the anniversary of his death and I found myself weeping: "Oh Peter! You took the biggest slice of life and love I've ever known. There was not much left of the cake when you decided to leave this world and let go. The spark was there in your eyes from the day you were born. The joy that you cried out burned brightly for all of us and yet no joy came to you. Strange darkness came into your life and it never seemed to leave you. You were so loved and a loving son so why did you have to die that way? Only one like you could hover in the depth of darkness and still give the gift of unselfish love. We are left with the pain of your parting and still wonder why you had to die that way. Perhaps I expected too much of you, pushing you beyond the things of youth. I thought I was doing the right thing as you displayed so much ability. In your final breath, did you think you had let me down? Is that why I alone was mentioned in your suicide note. I can hear those written words 'Dad, I am sorry I caused you so much pain?' Peter, there is no answer as to why you died in vain."

As I sat there in my contemplating, my heart ached for a moment longer with the memory of loss and I exclaimed: "I am letting go now, for I am old and worn and weary and I trust in God that one day I shall see you again and we can embrace as Father and Son." A sudden flash of memory of Peter putting his head on my shoulders as he so often did at the start of the day's activities and hearing him once more saying "What are we doing today big fellow?" Me sitting there listening to his plans for the future and those that had passed and always giving me some credit for his success: Listening to him share with others his vision but always including "My Father this and my Father that" in his statements. It was there I cried out to the mountain "Son, you will never leave this sad heart of mine and I will live with the thorn there until the day I die. I tried to drink the pain away, the loss of you, the loss of family, but it was all in vain. If you are looking now son, I haven't had a drink for many a long day and it's a day at a time without a drink for me now and it is in the hands of the God of my own understanding that I remain sober. If you're looking now my boy, you can be proud of me now, more than ever when you were alive, when I was a drinker." Somewhere in the back of my subconscious mind I heard the words of Bill Wilson the co-founder of Alcoholics Anonymous whispering "Deep down in every man, woman and child is a fundamental idea of God, it may be obscured by calamity, by prompt, by worship of other things, but in some form or other it is there. For faith in a Power greater than ourselves and miraculous demonstrations of the Power in human lives are facts as old as man himself." Bill had suffered much like I had suffered too and like him for a while alcohol had become his only friend. Like him a faith in a Higher Power greater than self had been the answer to a new found freedom and ever so slowly I was letting go my past life too. It was there in this melancholy state of mind and heart felt wound of my spirit that the Christ once more appeared briefly with a reminder of my duty for my remaining days.

I had a vision of him seated with many children and chastising his apostles that stood nearby with the words:"Suffer the little children to come unto me for of such is the kingdom of heaven. "Then he turned and looked towards were I was seated upon this rock on the Pyrenees mountains of the Camino way and it was a reminder of the duties of me and my fellowman in this age. Christ restated what he had long ago stated to the multitude : "But if anyone causes one of these little ones who believe in Me to stumble, it would be better for him to have a large millstone hung around his neck and to be drowned in the depths of the sea" (Matthew 18: 6).

Christ faded from view but his words echoed through my mind as I thought of the hand in the dark and its part in the still suffering children in third world poverty, of the millions taken into slavery and prostitution, of the many who suffer the torment of pedophiles, and of those who are maimed, blinded and lost in the war zones of our world. My mind puzzled as to what can and should be done to change the evil that inflicts such devastation on our children. My thoughts were interrupted by the appearance of the old man in full military uniform who had first appeared on my previous French route Camino. Major General, Count Cherep-Spiridovich, soldier, political activist, writer and visionary, once more appeared to me and reminded me of the work that I needed to continue to do in using my talents for the greater good. "I have returned to speak to you" he stated: "to encourage you to continue your writings to enhance the welfare of future generations by your experience and expertise, to encourage Christian souls to take their journey to the centre of their being with prayer and meditative practices." The Count's own lifetime of work advanced the cause to end the world wars of the 20th century, told of the evil of the hand in the dark and how prayer and meditative practices were essential to the survival of man and the opening up of God like knowledge to ensure the world turns to the ways of the Golden rule and not of satanic evil practices.

I listened intently once again as he recounted the development of the Secret Society of One World power and of one of its founding members Amschel Mayer, Godfather of the banking cartel of Europe and the Rothschild Empire. The Count reminded me of Amschel's famous statement "Give me control of a nation's money supply and I care not who makes the laws." He warned that there has never been a more dangerous time to live in the world of materialism than the present day. "Bankers print the money, bankers lend it all at exorbitant interest rates, bankers foreclose on those who have difficulty repaying and bankers eventually get all the money back with interest to boot. Learn to budget, learn to live with frugality and keep some powder dry for the tough times."

It was a fair warning as like most of my generation we lived for just another day on the gravy train of making a living, enjoying the fruits of our labour, rewarding ourselves with the material benefits of an affluent society. The first worlds societies awash with money, material possessions, affluence and prestigious influence whilst those of poorer nations suffered from the need for basic necessities for life, lacking the luxury of clean water, daily bread and adequate accommodation. Many had turned to a nomadic life, refugees moving from country to country in the hope that they may stay, work, make a living for their families and contribute to their new home and way of life. We of the long forgotten world of the Golden rule are far too preoccupied with ourselves, materialism and the distractions of the Hand in the Dark agenda to really bother with the fact that we are caught in the snare of a web of false prophets who are leading us down a dark passage towards an inevitable Armageddon if we don't wake up soon. "Cash is King" I hear the catch cry of the bankers of our world who finance us all for their own ultimate agenda and greed. Somewhere in the shadow of my subconscious mind I heard the small voice of that ancient Jewish banker cry out again "Cash is Emperor."

The old Count looked at me with knowing eyes, he had seen it all before in the Slavonic Society of Russia, the Latino- Slavic League of Paris, the British and the European Royal connections, the British system of Government and he gave me stark warning then and there. "Watch out for the signals from the Club of Rome's current day members who are manipulating the Governments and financial systems of the world for the coming One World Government agenda, the downfall of democracy and the rise of the one who will lead, the hand in the dark agenda for he who will rule, he will be known by that number 666." It was a stark warning and as he faded from view once more, I wished only to free my mind of the thought of money, materialism and world powers.

I tried to focus once again to meditate and get back to that free spiritual action that was the only way of relief for me in my sense of reality. Try as I may, the thought of the devastation that may await us all on this earthly plain in the not too distant future would not give me the peace of mind that I so richly desired and believed I deserved. The world had been torn asunder throughout its history by war and plagues and to a great degree domination by Church authority, dictators and bankers of all persuasions for their own agenda and prideful glorification and here I am, a lone pilgrim on a mountain top attempting to mediate and pray my way forward. A lone voice in the wilderness I thought, for no-one else seems to want to listen to the message that had been handed to me by The Count, the Christ, and the Prophets. Then suddenly as if by magic they were back with me and I heard the voices in the wilderness of my mind, it was the voices in unison of Daniel and John the Baptist crying out to me: "Trust in God, his Son and your Saviour, for if you believe he is ultimately the answer to your way from here on in, you will find he is the way, the truth and the light, and all will be well. If you but hand your will over to him and pray, the answers to your ultimate way will come to you." It was a tall order for me to do for I had forgotten how to pray, how to think, how to believe, for I had fallen so far into the dragon's mouth of creative ideas, that I had lost the plot to my reality of being. I could preach of the coming of an Armageddon, I could write songs of love, of joy, of darkness and of light, but was all of this coming from my head and not my heart? Somewhere deep inside I heard "Trust, let Go and leave it to God, for he understands you better than you can possibly ever imagine. He has a plan for you as he has always had for all of mankind ever since the beginning. The issue is with the dark side of your making and not the will of your Father of the Light, who is also within you. Stay clear of the forces of darkness for which you have so earnestly strived, it is time to work only for the glory of God. State your message clearly and precisely for you were born of goodwill not of evil deed and you, like all of your generation, have been conditioned to follow the dictate of your desires and not of your spirit. Don't be fooled by the world any longer, your task is to help those who are in need of your guidance and experience. Guide others to do likewise, to hand over to the Lord of the Light and not the hand in the dark. The way may not be clear to you yet but prayer and trust." The voices faded from my mind and I was once more alone on the mountainside and felt that I could now meditate.

Another figure of vast knowledge now appeared. . A tall gaunt John Maine of priestly order appeared to remind me that all I had to do was pray the mantra 'Mar- ra- na- tah,' focusing on the breath and the discipline of repetition and the spirit of the Christ would descend upon my soul and I would have what is most desired, spiritual freedom to act, see and do, with confidence within the bounds of what it is that the God of my own understanding has planned for me." I had tried every type off meditation that offered heightened awareness in my stress filled world were my senses had been dulled to follow the herd and not the dictates of my conscious self as I have been created to do. The Mar- ra- na -tha worked for a while and from time to time it may be beneficial in the future as my spiritual self dictates. However loving kindness mediations helped quell my feelings of anger, frustration and resentments as did the scanning of my body in guided meditation calm me. Mindfulness heightened my senses to remain aware and in the present moment and meditation of slow movement and visual - guided meditation gave me a key to unlock the subconscious.

John Maine faded from my presence, as I made my way from that high mountain place of the Pyrenees on my Camino. The journey of this way from the graveyard of my son had taught me the meaning of letting go. The Christ had given me the gift of love and understanding by his supreme sacrifice and I had to acknowledge despite my disbelief that there was much sacred belief and meaning in celebrating his death and resurrection for humanity as was taught to me as a child. It was not my Catholic upbringing so much as ritual actions and sacrifices of those who taught me to live in a Christ like way for the good of all concerned that now resonated. Those teachers of Christ who taught faith and good intent to willing children. Those self- same teachers who ruled with the caine and back handers to chisel free minds into some sort of community of soul still resonated. I had to overlook the shadows of those who carried their religious zeal too far. Perish the thought of the extremes of those who sexually abused the children of our time too. It was for the law and the Church to pursue each case of abuse on its merit and all I could do was let go.

I was on my sacred journey and felt compelled to recall my life in the world of the material, to pass on the wisdom of what I had learnt. It was up to the reader to evaluate if they wished to take on board my lesson of financial management that had been hard won in the world of investing and trading. The potential for an Armageddon had been foremost in my minding in the telling and that was my real motivation.

The realization that I was just as big a participant in taking the bait of the material avaricious and power and had become just another mouse on the wheel of debt in the palm of the bankers hands. I make no excuse for using the Rothschild banking family tree as my template of explaining the world of Elite banking power. I no longer have the wealth I once possessed in part to my own previous fault but I am no longer in the clutches of the bankers at this point in time either. I figured that now to be a good thing, for I have done the family thing, paid the price of the material devil, run a business and without the bankers I had to admit, I would not have achieved any of those goals. But there had to be a balance and it was only now in the wisdom of age that I had come to realize that my life was not over, my family had moved on and that was good. I had no excuse now but to do the duty of using my talents for however my Higher Power deemed for it for me to do.

I was on a new Camino and it was not the Camino de Santiago any more. it was the spiritual Camino of my life I was on and I looked forward with a spirit of 'ever onward' which had been part of my indoctrination as a child too. For a brief moment I was back in the 'Wicklow heather' pub, in the room with those great writers of the past and it was then I recalled the words I had read from a book of George Bernard Shaw. 'This is the true joy in life, being used for a purpose recognised by yourself as a mighty one. Being a force of nature instead of a feverish, selfish little clod of aliments and grievances, complaining that the world will not devote itself to make you happy. I am of the opinion that my life belongs to the whole community and as long as I live, it is my privilege to do for it what I can. I want to be thoroughly used up when I die, for the harder I work, the more I live. I rejoice in life for its own sake. Life is no brief candle for me. It is a sort of splendid torch which I have got hold of for the moment and I want to make it burn as brightly as possible before handing it on to future generations.'

My thoughts focused on nothingness as the straps from my backpack seemed to burn into my shoulder blades. I stopped long enough to relieve the weight off my shoulders before once more shouldering my pack and trudging the mountain track again. I had met so many pilgrims on The Way on past Camino adventures. They had stayed but for a while, communicating via social media until the novelty had worn thin. "Ships in the night" I told myself. I had attended a yoga session at the last village I stayed. It was an opportunity to get the aches and the kinks and pain out of my body before venturing on. Whilst in vacant and pensive mood, my thoughts drifted back to loves won and lost.

CHAPTER 8.

REMEMBER LOVES FLOWERS.

It only seems like yesterday we met in the garden of wildflowers It was there by the moon beams that we so often kiss, and everywhere I looked you were there gazing at me again with the fondness of affection. You gave me love there as the sky lightened to the warmth of the sun, and I could hear you sigh in the peaceful call of a bird on the wing, All along the sky shone in the twinkle of your eye, in the poetry on our lips, in the rhythm under the lights of the planets. We lay there in the grass looking at the wildflowers as the honeybees hummed through the lavender and the graceful butterfly flitted its colours about. In everything then as now I see your image, breath in your of nakedness in the nature of myself; in the landscape, the rivers, the stars as I tramp the night, the rolling fields of wheat in the wind that brings me back to the winds of my mortality. You have departed now like so many others whom I loved or at lest thought it so in my former life.

Yet in everything I can still see your image, hear your voice when in our flowering past we lay naked by the roses.You would hold me fast as long as it lasted, taking me home away home in the rhythm of your sighs. I was not so sensitive back then. I did not know the ways to drain from fortune's chalice the nectar of the love that comes from a women's touch. I still recall the story in stirring tones of our love that joined two souls as one in the murmur of the flowers, the kindred heart of the breeze that blew over the mild breath of the remindful plain.. Thoughts of sweet nothings in your ear and the fondness messed in the bed of grass created for you.The thrilling laughter and our child like voices whispering. And after it was over and we lay in each others arms, I searched the sky and traced the clouds in dreams of future treasures.

And how I recalled the symbols of the saints on the nearby graveyard, those days when I let out inspired verse beneath the sky, felt the rhythmical music of the soul as the waters pounded nearby rocks, the roar of thunder and the vision of lightning stretched across the sky. It was then I caught the ghost like image in your face as once more I took you home, drinking the elixir of the fragrance of your body in the afternoon once more. But no longer do you sit beside me by the roses, lie in the carpet grass and make love. No more will I kiss you as I have done a thousand time since with other women. Oh! I have lost the sense of harmonious motion once again. My heart aches for love but my spirit flags and my laughter is as cruel as Judas' smile. Now I take to my journey once more as pilgrim of the Way and the spirit. Everything has drifted on at last, drifted on like a feather that the sea carries back, defenceless against the tide and the life, the pleasant life it comes but it will be ours no more, no never more my love.

Today I trod with head held high where yesterday I trod with gaunt neck bowed low. The backpack is my lonely burden but I hear your rustic dress now trailing nearby in my imagining and walk in a daze dreaming of a life were the golden roses once bloomed. I freely devote my thoughts to captive memories of sweet lover, build whimsical castles in the air. I pass a pond were we once walked arm in arm. It was where you once used to lean and the moonlight rays would come to rest. I still believe I could feel, bearing my faith up with a prayer from behind a veil of solace. Embrace your devoted stone softening gaze from which led me long ago within love's prison. As I climbed another hill, the twilight of evening tide seemed to carry you towards me in the sound of your vibrant metallic voice. But it was an illusion, just the bold fragrance of sweet perfume from a nearby garden of lavender as I passed by. The sun's last mellow rays slid down into the dying throe, as I entered another small village of The Way. Church bells rang out with a slow severity calling believers to their biding.

 And as the night, the cool night enveloped me, I took from a flower patch near the church two purple columbines and wondered who, after I die might close my limp eyelids. I think as I walk arm in arm with another grim pilgrim of the way and I beg my latest love to accept that my existence will fade as I am old and not so strong as I once was, but I wish it not to end. Wish it to last forever, the passion of my blood through my veins, but life has to a great degree been cruel to me. I accept that and pray the grave may prove to be kinder to me than the life I have lived; for like all men of age we rage to the last of the fading light of loves gaze. But I, like all men go to the women to help ease the painful journey, bending to the pleasure that lures within her loins. The fairest of ladies with long and merciful gaze shall once more embrace and take with diving ember the last of the joy from the embers of my pain. For she will gaze upon me in my dying silence. I break the spell of this thought and consider that as I am in the afternoon of my life I should perhaps be turning to God of my joyful spirit of suffering for in the final hours it will be he not the loins that I shall be seeking. Yet I do not yet wish to leave this life, to fly the world and all its creatures, I will not yet seek to forsake this cruel and sorry life till the eve day on which the love in me shall die of you, the earth and nature's glory. And if you outlive me, you shall die of grief my family, my friends my lover, die of grief that I no longer live. For you shall not come to mourn me beside rustic blooms and water, tears of the ground of piteous weeds, but you will find me waiting there for you among the beds of flowers, the dahlias will be weeping in the jasmines' arms!

And for this as I write my journal of this new way, I shall sum up on loves epitaph. Love it is said makes the world go round. There are numerous myths which tell of passion and repulsion, marriage and separation, love and rivalry, sexual fidelity and infidelity, and the transcendent power of compassion underlining the cental importance of love in our lives. I have lived and loved in a world of mythology. I've lived the complexity of the morality which myth presents as equal multifaceted. There is no greater puzzle than the mystery of why people are attracted or repelled by each other, and we often seek simple answers to questions which require a stretching of the soul to formulate opinion and much less an answer to its mystery. The loves and sorrows of the myth of love comes in many shapes and colours and some are distinctly exotic. Despite the fact that my life stories may challenge many moral assumptions about relationships, myth about love can also offer solace in our unhappiness, guidance in our dilemmas, and sorely needed insights into why we sometimes create the dilemmas in our personal lives.

Sexual passion is portrayed as a force more powerful than any other, capable of driving humans into actions against their will and better nature, often ending in tragedy. The Gods and Goddesses of myth often afflict men and women with uncontrollable passion, bringing a kind of madness and destruction on those who offend. Yet passion itself is not portrayed as a negative or immoral force. It is allied with strength, courage, sexual potency and the soul's response to beauty; it reflects the power and tenacity of life force itself; and because it is god-inspired, it is sacred. Myth teaches us that it is the manner in which mortals pursue their passions, and the degree to which passion overwhelms consciousness, that are the real sources of hurt rejection and even catastrophe. The eternal triangle of relationships are always the essence ingredients of great poetry, drama and fiction, as well as many lawyer's income of which I well know from personal experience. Infidelity hurts and demeans us; but it is also fascinates us, perhaps because we know it's sufferings and enchantments as well. The eternal triangle is an archetypal experience, and psychology is full of expirations about why we stray. We know from bitter experience that loss of trust corrodes marriage and destroys family life; and deceit makes us feel humiliated. It is the betrayal of the greatest human sufferings one can imagine. Yet we know little why mankind seeks monogamy and enacts polygamy then when the greater myth of sexual and emotional betrayal were first written down. So it is that I turned to express my thoughts on love in poetry as I walked my new way of living the myth of love, of betrayal, of death, living the poetry of its mystery, myths and the reality of love, of lustful deception and despair. The lessons came fast and furious for me and without fear nor favour I gave way to expressing of poetry to relieve me of the pain and suffering as I walked on the Camino de Santiago and in expresses my emotions on paper, on my tales of life and on the Wicklow Way.
Love.

Is it the sound I'm hearing in the trees
do I see you in the falling leaves
maybe it's the sweetness of the breeze
the feel of sand between my toes.

We did our loving in some distant past
life was always splendour in the grass
now feelings are faded memories
and nothing ever lasts for long.

Is it the body cradled in my arms
the warmth of her constant charms
maybe it's the child upon my lap
that sense of innocence.

Oh! love,
come back into my room
and take away these blues.

Did I see you in the corner of my eye,
the shadow of a bird flying by
the warmth of the sun upon my face
maybe now in a fading cloud,

Did I see you somewhere on the road
was it a gentle hand upon my back
maybe it's the burden of the load
when I am looking back.

We came together staring into space
listening to the sound between the words
dancing our way together in the rain
then we just died in tune.

Oh! Love
come back into my room
and take away these blues.

Now I'm here out upon the track
walking with my knapsack on my back
taking the rough with the smooth
looking for the love that I once knew.

Are you there with the man in the moon
did I see you in a shooting star
the flash of light in star studded sky
that faded out too soon.

Yesterday we did cartwheels on high
laughed a lot until we said goodbye
and the wheel is still in spin
hoping you will return again.

Oh! love
come back into my room
and take away these blues.

We came together staring into space
listening to the sound between the chords
dancing our way together in the rain
then we just died in tune.

Now I'm here out upon the track
walking with my knapsack on my back
taking the rough with the smooth
looking from the love that I once knew.

Did I see you somewhere on the road
was it a gentle hand upon my back
maybe its the burden of the load
when I am looking back.

Oh! love
come back into my room
and take way the blues.

The track had narrowed and I followed the river not knowing where I
was and cared little for the place I was in my minds eye. I just looked
forward to the next place to take a meal, get freshened up and rested.
The track widened again and I found myself wandering by a field with
peach and plum trees in full fruit. It was an orchard of a great variety
tomato vines, grapes hanging like breast to feed upon and a reminder
of home with a cain sugar growing nearby. I ate my fill and grabbed a
couple of plums for later. I passed an old house near a village. An old
lady was sitting by the gateway eating an apple. She looks up at me
with a smile and passed me one to eat. I accepted and once again
she smiled, went over to a nearby tree and picked a couple more offering them to me for my journey. I thanked her with a typical Spanish
acknowledgment, turned and waved my hat with a sense of gratitude.

Humanity can be so generous at times and I knew God was in the heavens for me that day. I was on the Portuguese route from Lisbon to Santiago and it was a mid summer memorable day.

It was four days on the trails after leaving the sad city of Lisbon in decay. My mind drifted back to my arrival there. . The signs of the city in the depth of an economic turndown and the strain on the faces of the people in the streets reflected despair and misery. On arrival by bus from the airport, I made my way to a cafe for coffee and a sandwich before heading off to my hotel. I was reminded of the once thriving city rich in mythical traditions, folklore, literature and preserved ancient monuments, all of which spoke the legends of the past, for it turned out that is all that remained for the people of the city and Portugal at large really. These people still cling to the traditions of myth, legends and folklores and supernatural beings who live in the forest amid the rising waters of the sea and on the sandy beaches. The whole nation is dumbed down by the three Fs- Football, Fardo and Fatima. The old folk just sat around cafes and bars watching the soccer on tv, listening to morbid Faro music of mournful tunes and lyric. They tell tales over coffee of the past life they lived, of sea or the life of the poor and the miracles of Fatima. They seemed to come alive on local saints feast days or when a famous Portuguese bullfighter came to town, then only to return to their slumber of inertia and conditioning when those days were over. It had seemed to me at the times there was to be but a few rays of hope on my Portuguese journey. I was walking in a vacant landscape of a people who had just given up. It was as thus I entered that cafe on that fate filled morning on my 2015 Camino.The place was not busy despite it being peak hour in the centre of the city. The waitress with friendly greeting had taken note of my heavy backpack still on my shoulders and had asked where I was bound for. " Oh!" I had said " Another Camino" She brightened up even more and said she would come with me if I wanted her too. I laughed and she said: "Señor, I like your smile, I could be your women if you want." I had thought how desperate things must be for a young women to give herself so freely. She may well have been joking, so I replied " Thank you, but you're not my type." I could still hear her laughter as I took my coffee and sandwich to an outside table to eat, drink and enjoy the sunshine.

Behind the facade of street peoples faces stood ancient decaying buildings whose inner beauty was kept alive with fresh paint whilst the outer walls were badly in need of repair. The only buildings that seemed to be maintained were Government funded. The museums' Museum de Lisboa are a chain of old museums across town that displayed the history from prehistoric times to modern day. Full of beautiful paintings and ancient craft that depicted the history of Lisbon as a foreigner might see it. A coin of the realm of Julius Caesars' head on one side and another of Alexander the Great in full military dress featured campaigns across this region. They were different Monarchs for different times but not so different in death, for the 'Grim Reaper' once more got this reward and all that's left are coins to remind us of the lessons of a distant past. There was no history of the Portages man of Wars, The Caravel nor the Spice Trade or of their great hero " Henry the Navigator" who apparently had not ventured forth into battle or ventured to the sea because he could not swim and was afraid of the water. The museum reeked of the history of Roman conquest, The Moors, The Spanish and the English, but little of what made this city famous; nothing of the poets, philosophers, musicians, artists, and the greatest of Monarchists. The Architects who built this fine city and those of intellect and creative pursuit that had changed it's face were nowhere to be seen; all but faded like ashes to ashes. It seemed to me there was more reality of the historic Lisbon as viewed from the street than in the walls of the museums. It may well of been my mood but I did not leave the museum inspired by the history of Lisbon.

Already the ladies of the night were hanging about the street eyeing off the better dressed men in the hope of draining their vital fluids and extracting money from their wallets. Young men were still dancing in the square as they had been doing all day and children in some tradi- tional native costumes were dancing too. Middle aged men played guitars and a young boy with a drum beating time, all competing for the tourist Euro. This was the way of an ancient city in a modern world of battling masses of people in quiet desperation. My mind returned to the path I walked in Spain. I had similar feelings when I walked the Camino this time and on my journey in Ireland too. Though this Lisbon experience was a part of my Camino, there were no flowers in the field. I recall feeling a little bit sad, a bit lost back then. I had walked back in time, an attempt to view Lisbon from a different prospective, walking the city as if I was walking the Camino, photographing local scenes, recording the voices of the singers and music of the street. It was like pressing fresh flower petals between the pages of a book or putting flowers in bloom in a jug, only to see them later wither and die; living today and dead in the morrow, A space in time off just another day in the life. I turned my mind to contemplate love.

I had come to this foreign land to find my way back to spirituality; back on a new but ancient road to Santiago. This at least I told my- self, but in truth I just wanted to get laid again. Luisa, the good doctor I had met on Facebook before I left Australia had invited me to meet her in Lisbon. She had planned to show me around the city and its surrounds before I ventured north on the Portuguese way to Santiago. Luisa said her practice was very busy, but she had to plan time away to follow me. I knew she wanted to make love by the time I was ready to depart the city. She had said she needed a week to get things in order and she would meet me in Porto, the famous port wine city were the name Port wine originated., She had planned to walk The Way with me as far as the border between Portugal and Spain. Typically she put up a protest to test me. Her words were that she was interfering with my spiritual path on the Camino. I waved that aside quickly with a retort; " Oh, it's o.k. I've walked The Way before." My mind drifted back to that last day in Lisbon before I left on my journey to a temporal pathway to getting my rocks off.

True to her word Luisa was waiting outside my hotel door to drive me about for a last short tour around the city. An overview of things to come with her was exciting as she drove through the streets of the old capital to the outskirts of Lisbon and the continuance of my Camino. Before leaving the outer Lisbon, Luisa had driven me up to the mountain side to view an old ruin. We stood together at the remaining structure, an observation point in the old world to gaze to a distant mountain were another temporal castle stood some 30k north as the crow flies to another Templars castle high above a rivera, an entry vantage point with a view to the Atlantic ocean making it a perfect place to protect Lisbon and surrounds from approaching enemy forces. A parting visit to the walled city of Evora appeared like it was rising from the plains as Luisa drove to its gateway entrance. There we took pleasure in the local victuals of pork and wine lunch. Driving slowly, we made our way east of Evora through corkwood forest to the cave of Escoural. The 15,000 year old cave drawings had me returning in my mind to thoughts of the Aboriginal caves, known to be over 50,000 years old that dotted Australia, drawing devotion to the Gods. The impressions of ancient peoples of Portugal as in my homeland made me more determined to continue my investigation into myth, legends and folklore of the Camino.

Luisa stopped the car at the edge of the city and we stood for a long time kissing intensely. Our embrace was broken by the 'toot toot' of the horn of a passing semi trailer. Truck drivers always like the wild and the alternate life style as their big wheels turn on their own chosen way of life. I shouldered my backpack and took a last look back at Luisa on the other side of the Expressway. We both waved a final good bye as I began my tramping. I was once more a happy wanderer making my way along the track for my next adventurer of myth, legends and folklore and the promise of loved mystery in the future.

CHAPTER 9.

A LITTLE MORE SUNSHINE

The majority of mankind choose nothing but the world and seem to suffer even more as consequence as I have done in the past. I was different now travelling in a meditative state with every step on this Portuguese Camino I seemed to be on a spiritual plain hanging without fear to the reality of this world. In the corners of my mind there seemed to be a way leading from the loss of a kind that sorts illusion from reality. I could not quite put my finger on it but justified it all in my mind on the road I travelled, on this manifestation of a life journey, with all its sham, drudgery and broken dreams. I reasoned somehow that the spiritual path I was on was always meant to be. I heard my mind ticking over the thoughts of sacrifice and deprivation in the hope of a spiritual enlightenment, but also realised that such a path is to nowhere, another illusion. More instructions came from the beyond as each step was an instruction, like being guided into knowing that I was being taken care of, but maybe it was just a mind thing, another illusion. Then again maybe it was God talking to me or the ego workingas counsel. I had to consider myself not to be tempted to walk ahead of truth and accept illusion and reality as one and the same- just to trust and let each step of the way be the roadmap. But what   really was the Camino about for me now? Was it that I would uncover the meanings of myth of the Camino and the lessons from people's lives lived along this backwood road. The living of the many steps to Santiago was just as much a step back in time, faith and truth for me as it was facing up to myself, the reality that pain is good so to speak for it makes us strong for future battles as well as the present ones.

The evening was closing in and the sun had disappeared beyond the horizon, the air was dry and the heat still stifling. Walking along quiet country lanes, across farm tracks and back again. It was a challenge as there were no markers to guide me; not like the well-marked route of the' French' Camino across the Pyrenees . I was out of food and almost out of water but content to accept what fate had in store for me. It was around 9 p.m. when I walked on a cobbled stone byway with sparsely scattered houses to my left and an agricultural canal to my right. Old street lights glowed a lonesome invitation in the semi -darkness and the only sign of life was a light in a cafe bar still open. There were old men and middle aged farmers still in their working clothes seated in front of a TV watching a bullfight, not an unusual sight, except for the fact that they were outside on a dusty pavement sitting on weather worn chairs with eyes glued to an equally old tv set propped up on a wooden box for better viewing. They seemed to be lost in the moment as the sound of ' El Toro?' screamed from the box. Either the TV didn't work inside and this was the best place for a clear reception or it was far too hot seated in a small crowded bar. A poster on the bar wall detailed the festivities planned for the weekend. A bull-fight was to be the star attraction showing a picture of the fated mata-dor, the Portuguese Ana Maria. She was the most famous of all living bullfighters in Spain and Portugal, took risks beyond other bull fight-ers putting her body without defence into the line of the charging bull's horns, only to move at the last moment. It was a flirt with death and every time she did that the crowd roared as did the Spanish blood fire across both nations. My mind snapped back to the reality of the present moment, as I passed the poster of hero Ana Maria jousting with a bull. It had also been on the wall of a small bookshop in San Domingo de la Calzada. It had been at the point of that first Camino journey that I had decided to buy a "village to village" guide book of the Camino. At the time I had been lost once already on the Way and reckoned a guide map was then needed. I regretted that I had no map for this Portuguese Camino to Santiago to guide my way. The old lady waitress at the cafe bar made me a a fresh sandwich of ham, cheese and tomato. It was the only food available apart from beer and coffee.

It was highly unlikely that I would find a place to lie my weary head but I enquired of the old women behind the bar in the hope whether she knew of a place I could stay for the night. There was little chance of that as it was just a sparsely populated road siding with a couple of houses, a few storage sheds and the cafe bar. The kindly old lady busied herself on the phone looking for a place for me. I waited out-side the bar with the crowd of bullfight viewers, eating the remainder of the sandwich and drinking my coffee just waiting. Before long an English speaking Portuguese man, a little worse for wear from booz-ing appeared. He told me that the old lady had spoken to the priest in the next village some 2.5 km down the road. He advise that if I en-quired at the rectory they would find me a bed for the night. Thanking the old lady and the kindly boozed up English speaking Portuguese man, I made my departure. The viewers of the bullfight never once met my gaze; they were far too busy fighting the bull that appeared on the old tv set.

I did my best to wake the dead as I banged on the church door. It was a white stucco building with an attached hall and large timber door. The sound echoing back when I knocked was hollow. I noticed a nearby building in the church grounds, and made my way to the front door then hammered on it a few times in rapid repetition. A young well built, obviously German youth, appeared in his undies. Judging by his bare chest and broad shoulders, he would have been an ideal recruit for the Hitler youth; for he was blond, blue eyed and appeared athletic. He gruffly ask what I wanted and Initially he refused my re-quest for a place to stay but softened when I explained that the old lady from the next village had phoned the priest who promised me a bed for the night. The youth asked me to wait explaining that the priest was playing cards at a near by house with local parishioners and he would go checkout my story. He returned ten minutes later with the biggest metal key I had ever seen in my life.

We made our way to the building next to the church and he injected the key into a slot in the door and it creaked its way open. Turning on some lights, a majestic hall appeared like an apparition out of the darkness. Its was a function centre and gymnasium all in one. The German youth bid me a good evening and vanished. I locked the front door from within and surveyed the surrounds. The only possible bed was a vaulting horse in one corner as it had a leather padding on top. I lay out my sleeping bag, did my toiletries in a newly built bathroom noting that it had a new shower installed. Returning to my metre high bunk, I was asleep within a matter of seconds. A long shower and an-other reshuffle of my backpack revealed the headlamp had lodged in the very front corner of the bag. Its black outer casing is no doubt why I could not find it the night before in the dark. I had walked the 2.5 Km like a blindman in the dark to the church door. Considering I had been walking on a track between fields of crops it was a small wonder I did not tread on a reptile and got myself bitten. I thanked God for his guidance in that matter, made a pencil note on my Credential del Peregrine, proof of my nightly stay on the Camino and a record for the Compostela Certificate I would receive on completion of this Camino in Santiago. The remainder of my tramp I would ensure a stamp was placed on the passport by the proprietors of places I stayed as a guaranteed proof of the way of my journey.

The morning was alive with colour as I traversed the flow of sown lands, passing vines of grape, berries, apples and plum trees. The market gardens of Portugal enriched by the alluvial soil of the Tejo River narrowed to a more intimate one. The Way changed course to a tarred road and I walked to the sound of my walking poles tapping on the hard surface of the road. By mid-morning I had made it to Porto de Muge for two large black coffees-the tar of Portugal! The cafe had only bread rolls to eat, but it was wholesome enough to sustain me until a more appropriate cafe could be found. Outside the cafe I en-countered my first Pilgrim on a bike who assisted me with directions. We said our " Buen Camino" and parted company. From there,I me-andered my way on sandy tracks with changing fields of crops being my only guide posts.

I had walked the Way of a worn track on a fertile plain following the Rio-Tejo River to a steep climb into the   historical city of Santarem. The Templar Castle that appeared at a turn in the river sat on an al-most island like hill at the edge of the river. It was virtually impossible to gain entry by land to the site. Asking directions, I followed a thick bush track along the edge of the river that opened to a roadway and carpark.Tourists had left their cars and climbed down a steep cliff to a boat ramp below. The boatman was quick to charge two euros for each passenger on his small boat crossing of some 100 metres to the waters edge near the Castle that loomed high above the river. It was far too deep to wade across and besides, tourists had plenty of money in his eyes. I was tempted to leave my backpack on the river edge, wade out, then swim the 100 metres but thought better of it. I figured I may save two euros and lose my backpack to some spying eyes in the nearby brush. The Castle strutted out of a rocky edge island covered in small bush and white flowers. It was a majestic sight of light brown stone securing all around the high walls with holes window views to see up the river and other holes for cannons. High above that was an observation tower. As we tourists made our way up the long narrow track to the entry, I thought how difficult it would have been for the Knights Templar in full armour with sword and shield to climb that steep precipice. Indeed it would have been a deterrent for an invader too. As to the Castle entry it was far too wide but low. I had to stoop to go under the top of the doors which had me realise these Templars were not tall men. The Castle had limited sleeping quarters and more rooms for food storage, an armoury, gun powder for the cannons and cannon balls for firing at approaching invaders by sea. A panoramic vista up and down the the river and approach from the ocean to the mouth of the river was in full view. It was an ideal location to warn troops camped on the nearby shore below of approaching enemies and to send smoke signals to the townships along the river's edge warning of approaching invaders and to far off Templar castles which could be sighted on a near horizon. A networking ideal to rally support against any large energy force approaching by sea.

I made my way back along the river track to a Kiosk, purchased a coffee and a bight to eat. It was a perfect place with canopy shade to keep out the heat. A cool place to rest before continuing my Camino. The thought to hire a boat to traverse this side of Rio Tejo and explore the township on the opposite shore crossed my mind. In my facet mood I was distracted by the two young women busily serving tourists at the counter of the kiosk. Nearby was a slightly portly but athletic Portuguese man possibly in his early forties. He was doing little work but talked to the customers as they entered and exited the area. The friendly Portuguese raconteur entered the canopy enclosure and sat down to chat with me. It didn't take much prompting to tell his life story, as he began to chat in English. He told of the history of the area, his life as boatman before setting up this kiosk. Before long one of the young women approached him with a tone of anger in her voice. He waved her away and said to me that I was luckier than him, for I was free of the burden of business. More to the point he stated that the two women were his mistresses and the women on the other end of the phone was his wife.

Robo had introduced himself earlier and returned after the phone call with his wife with another coffee for me. He repeated in English "Women, are more trouble than they are worth." In his case with the three to contend with I had to agree.

Robo began to sprout his Templar knowledge of the local Knights, of the river and his family connections to the great feats of those Knights. He indicated that it was they who possibly held the secret to the Holy Grail, the Arc of the Covenant and vast treasures of gold and silver. It was they, he reckoned, who had taken to sea in eighteen ships to avoid it all falling into the hands of the French during the reign of King Philip. He said the Templar took not only vast wealth but great knowledge, wisdom and power for their future establishments throughout Europe and Britain. It was the Knights that introduced the basis of modern day banking, gathered great wealth, financed wars and fought many crusades for King, Pope and Country in their time. Of course, in Robo's story of the Knights they were all his ancestors and they knew how to keep women in check he stated with much admiration. The sun was lowly descending on the horizon as I said my goodbyes. "You re free my friend whilst I am burdened with this thing." He pointed to his penis and laughed aloud. I could hear the women still nagging him as I made my way back to the track. In the distance I heard a final call "Buen Camino foreign adventurer," he cried.

The quintessential medieval town of Tomar was the epitome of the most perfect example of a Templar layout and architecture I had seen on this journey. As I walked the town centre I was taken by the number of Medieval buildings that stood in pristine condition. The streets were busy with everyday merchants selling their wares. There were masses of tourists that had arrived as they had done in the Middle Ages. I was in a time warp back with the Templars and the village folk of medieval Portugal. Standing high on a hill above the town, the Templar Castle occupying a commanding location near the convent of Christ. Successive Grand Masters helped to plan great discoveries during there in the Age of Discovery when Tomar was then the centre of commerce for the Spice trade. The tourist information centre advised me that Pai, the founder of Tomar was buried in a tomb on the riverside where a quiet stream ran through the middle of the town. Walking by the river I got to thinking of the nature of evolution of towns and cities, from Neolithic evolution of the hunting and gathering natives to the marked transition of sowing and cultivation. The complexity of towns and cities seemed to emerge from a gathering of peoples under rulers and protection of the Knights historically. Well at least in Europe. Templar fortresses overlooked the town folk who grew crops for survival rather than to hunt for food. My mind was always awash with thoughts and ideas , for I was never content just to be like an everyday tourist viewing the sights. I just needed to know more about Tomar.

The town was constructed inside the walls of the Convento de Cristo, under the order of Gaualdim de Eris, the fourth Grand Master of Templar in the late 12th century. It grew to become the centre of international expansion under the Grand Master Henry 'The Navigator,' the successor to the Templar Knights of Portugal. The city was built over ruins of a Roman city built under Augustus Caesar's reign. When the Templars were banned for heresy throughout Europe in 1314 under the pressure of Pope Clement V, the Portuguese King Denis persuaded the new Pope John XX11 to allow fugitive Templars to join a newly created Order of Christ which Henry led. It was between 1384 an 1469 Prince Henry 'The Navigator' used the resources and knowledge of the Order of Knights to improve and add construction to the Convent of Christ. Henry gave orders for dams to be built and swamps to be drained. As a result the township started to attract sellers and streets were designed in a rational geometrical fashion that still stand today. A new nave was added to the Convent of Christ in early Manueline architectural style. A Gothic style Church of St John the Baptist' was also built in similar Manueline style facade in the centre of the town .Later in 1557 additions to the convent of Christ was built under the successor D.Joao 111 and was considered the best of Renaissance architecture in all of Portugal. So the Convent of Christ, the Templar Castle on the hill and many other famous buildings that dotted the landscape of Tomar, saw the township expand during the Age of Discovery through to the 18th century. In time, like all houses of cards, the Templar castle of Tomar collapsed into ruin and obsolescence as did the Order that inhabited it. Or did it? To my imagination the restored Castle I visited and the beautiful township buildings looked much like they did at the height of the Templar Knights.

Seated opposite the Church of St. John the Baptist, I gazed to its white-clay walls, marvelling at the Gothic portal and eight voided Manueline towers, as I ate the customary cheese, olive and bread washing it down with strong Portuguese coffee. Sipping away at a second cup, I enjoyed the calm Portuguese pulse of the townspeople, viewing the vista with every beat of my heart. I strolled down a narrow marble cobbled stone street to the river viewing the yellow and red brick houses etched in time. Walking on, I came to an organic market garden in the public square drawn to the sound of the sad Fardo music that echoed through the open areas of the square and bounced off walls. I made my way through a garden of flowers and began the climb up the hill to the Templar Castle. Nearing the top I stopped at a pink blossom tree. It was reportedly on a tree like this that Judas had hung himself after selling Jesus for thirty pieces of silver. Pausing long enough to recall Jesus's utterance: "the one who betrays me, it would be better if he had never been born" and then: " Go. Do what you must do." Gazing on the beauty of the blossom tree, I shook off all thoughts of suicide and crucifixion.

I continued to climb the hill nearing something majestic, mysterious and unique of the Templar Grand Masters of Europe. In the corridor, of the tomb of Alvarez de Fre, where the infamous administrator of the village lay, I read the history engraved at the base of his stone casket. He had no doubt regularly walked the great tunnel from the centre of St. John the Baptist church in Tomar square below to the Castle chambers to petition the Knights for favours for the villagers. It is known that he wrote three petitions a week to the Knights Templar and they are buried in his tomb walls forever. Some consider that the wall of his tomb contains the location of the Ark of the Covenant and the Holy Grail itself. Others had written of secret maps tucked away within other Knight's burial tombs, supposedly great secrets from a time before even America was discovered. Such secrets of the Templar's possessing important maps etched within the architecture of the many window frames and walls of the Castle was part of my goal for the journey. To find the secret behind a caravel ship which was wreck off the coast of Victoria during the Spice Wars in the Age of Discovery was a grand mission. The wreck of a caravel discovered in the late 19th century by an explorer in Australia was in itself amazing but no records of its history or how it came to be uncovered in the sands hills of a Victorian beach is still a mystery. It was well known that the Templar had designed the caravel ships for the rewards of transporting Spices from distant places during the Age of Discovery.

Now in the Castle of these great Templar Knights who designed the ships for the great seafarers of old, I was hoping to find an answer to the dilemma. Looking more closely at the carved stone images on the walls I recognised sunken ships within the rust brown algae, chains, buoys, swords, ropes and cables. Carvings I viewed of sailors knotted ropes, belts and clips with many other hidden messages to tell. Whilst I found all this to be fascinating, I was no closer to finding the answer to my mission of a Caravel that had washed up as a wreck of an Australian coastline beach. It had been known as the Mahogany ship because of the wood by which it had been built and I did not know at the time, but it would later lead tome to writing a book centred around its mystery. It lay like so many other symbols and myths within the walls of the great Castle. Henry 'The Navigator' had not only organised the Templars of Tomar but had sponsored and organised the voyages too. Though he never sailed the seven seas himself, his memory lasts in statues to his seafaring ambitions. Passing by wild orange trees in the main court yard, I remembered the seeds of such trees were imported to Southern Europe. Those same sweet oranges could be traced back to the Persian Empire, the Greeks, the Bulgarians, the Turks and the time of the Arabian Knights.

Before leaving Tomar I made my way below the Mayor's office and found a museum of old parchments in a glass protective casing. It was there I happened upon a parchment paper with the records of lost ships during the Age of Discovery. The words were worn and hard to decipher, but the Portuguese attendant who spoke English was most helpful.There were only two ships lost at sea in the vicinity of Australia bound for the Indonesian spices trade. Could it be that I happened upon the record of the "Mahogany Ship" as the Australian wreck came to be known? There was no visible date that could be deciphered on the old faded parchment, but at the time its was the only evidence I could rely upon to keep my interest in my imaginary goal.

I made my journey back to The Way with fond memories of the 12th century township, the peace in the parkland beside the quiet flowing river, the church of John the Baptist and the imposing Templar Castle on the hill with its mysteries of the past, and a mythical journey and the present day. Walking on this third Camino, looking back on those days in Tomar two years prior, the words of a humble motto of the Templar Knights came to mind: " Not unto us O Lord, but unto your name great glory." I was thinking then of self gratification and the horrifying condition of our ego oriented world making me likewise blind to the source of my true self identity. Such memories of my defects of character returned to haunt me. Bill Wilson, the co founder of Alcoholics Anonymous had fought hard to develop humility and wrote words in the twelve steps and traditions of AA to mirror what we may strive for: "….we are to practice a genuine humility. This is the end that our great blessings may never spoil us; that we shall forever live in thankful contemplation of Him who presides over us all." This to me was much like the journey of The Way I was on and the code of the Templar Knights stayed ringing in may head.

The roadway changed surfaces under my feet as I tramped tarred roadways, farm tracks, town pavements, old Roman roads, wooded pathways in forests of green and lonely country back lanes. My aim to leave the past behind me and traverse The Way that was no longer my way, but hopefully an outward covenant within my own Holy Grail of a narrow onward search. Like all my Camino journeys, the pathway to the Spirit always proved to be inward. It was never meant to be easy, and whilst most pilgrims suffered the physical pain of blistered feet and shin splints and the occasional dehydration, I never met a Pilgrim in any of my Camino ways that gave up the ghost before completing their own goals on their Camino. Many had external objectives in walking The Way, but my own quest for this journey ached with the inner desire for answers to my own fulfilment, only I did not realise it at the time. The artificial goal was ever present; it was the 'Mahogany Ship,' mystery that enchanted me to strive ever onward in the moment, but this myth in itself was a mask to my deeper self meaning for my existence.

I was back in present time on a different Way once more. The road to Santiago in the Meseta, with a vista of lush wheat fields before me, greened from recent rains maturing from the next harvest. This was a starkly different reality to the previous journey across this ancient landscape. It was mid-summer then, hot, dry and parched earth was all that greeted me. My vision crossing the desert in my constant plodding of the earth had my mind return to the journey from Tomar to Porto in 2015.

Approaching Porto the road network became very congested as I made my long slog into the city on hard city pavement. I was relieved to arrive at the city after a dangerous manoeuvring near fast moving traffic and unreasonable undulating terrain. Arriving at Porto, I made my way to the centre of the city and found a cheap rundown hotel to rest my weary head. A quick shower and I was back on the street again readily searching out this port city before nightfall. The fascination of this ancient city crammed full of old monuments, museums and despite an economic recession, a still busy shipping port. I was pleased that I had elected to stay a couple of days. Equally to enjoy the sites as much as the expectations of Luisa's arrival. She had texted me that she would arrive on the evening train and I visioned making love with her soon after. Knowing that she planned to travel on the road with me to complete this Camino de Santiago on the Portuguese Way gave me more excitement than the thought of a spiritual journey ahead. It was no longer a Camino of the soul but rather a Camino of misguided passion. She was devoted to the inner spirit and feared she had interfered with mine. I had protested as passion had already gripped me then back in Lisbon. I assured her that it was Okay. If only I had some forethought about an unfounded relationship that could not possibly work as we both had conflicting ideals, but I was blinded by the fever of sexual desire.

 Luisa had justified her interruption of my spiritual quest stipulating in a text that a Camino is just an illusion. She backed this up by referencing an Italian poet's statement by " Pilgrim, there is no answer, there is no way... cast a stone upon the water... watch the wake trails to the shore ... they fade and die. " It had prompted me to write a similar poem as I made my way around the museums and coffee haunts awaiting Luisa' arrival. In amounting of extreme passion, Luisa and I consummated our love rights. She had arrived on the evening train. we consumed a quick meal and then like ravenous animals made our way through the busy streets of Porto to the rundown hotel and into bed. There we quickly naked and entwined into a binding sexual embrace began to release our passions. The honeymoon period had began or should I say the honey trap. Suffice to sadly say that I was looking forward to our time together on The Way to Santiago, but it came to an abrupt end by the time we reached the border with Spain. I was keen to impress her with our love making and my over all brilliance. It was all mythical thinking on my part and whilst she told me on many occasion "I think I love you" that too was just a myth. Thinking I could produce incredible feats for her benefit, I sold her on my ideas" for our future but it was all mythical thinking on my part. It was not helped by her "on again off again" emotional turmoil and constant 'glass half empty' approach to life. I had enough of that in my former life and ultimately deeply regretted ever getting emotionally and physically involved with her. We parted on the Portuguese-Spanish border in not so pleasant circumstance. I did take a brief detour at the end of my then Camino, flew back to Lisbon to spend some emotional recovery time together and to see if we could patch things up again, but in the end that experience proved a disaster too. If we had just remained friends and not allowed our passions to get the better of us, we may well have had a lifelong friendship. We both had interest in travel, the arts, reading similar books and poetry and had an affinity with health and wellness. Not enough to make a lasting relationship of it though. My constant seeking of a prototype of my own conception had always been unachievable, mythical, and an unattainable goal verging on the spiritual. It had seemed to work for many years of my early married life but ultimately it came unstuck there too.

God and I crossed the desert wasteland and reached the village of Hosannas. I was greeted at the counter of the hostel by host Manuel and his love partner who both bid me welcome. He was a true Barcelona born Catalonian, spoke street Spanish and was naturally fluent in his native tongue. As for English, it was passable. "Hi, I am Manuel, the same name as the character in Fawlty Towers but with better service." He laughed loudly with a big grin on his dial and showed me to my room, advising that dinner would be served in about one hour. It was time enough for me to shower, change my clothing and sit in the courtyard to watch the flow of pilgrims tramp by and listen to those chating of their experiences of their day on the road.

It had been a night of strange dreams, a memorable dinner the evening before and a round table of pilgrims from all over the world enjoying the fruits of the land of Spain. Manuel had encouraged us to communicate with each other by having each dinner guest introduce themselves, identifying what country they came from and tell a little as to why they were walking the Camino. He was a grand host and told of his Camino story, sang a song and gave us all a piece of advice of a spiritual nature for our individual journey. It proved not to be unlike the homely of the priest at the Cathedral of Santiago when speaking at the Pilgrim's Mass I thought. Maybe Manuel had listened to a similar message from the priest there too. It was enough to later prompt me to write a song centred around his spiritual message.

The township of Hosannas was fading into the wilderness as I made my slow tramp on the Camino towards Santiago. Not far from the edge of town a young Belgium woman of mid to late thirties caught up with me and thus began an unforgettable journey together for a day on The Way. Like a Namatjira landscape, a watercolour of authenticity, this plain of ancient sacred knowledge echoed in the pastoral vision before my eyes. I felt a contentment and happiness as a weary wanderer, pleased once more to have the company of a young Goddess to share the spiritual highs I felt on this road to Santiago. We talked of love, of art, of photography, of loves lost and won, of the now and the spirit world beyond. Sabrina was free of much of what drove the material world and was doing her best to stay grounded despite her sensuality of which she freely spoke. We shared our food together, stopped for a coffee and tasted the locally baked cakes and bread whenever we took a break. These sugar delights were alway a common denominator of temptation on the Camino. This lady of Belgium spoke beautiful English with a twist of her native tongue. She took frequent photos of her surrounds and seemed to see things in nature that was not visible to man or beast, for every photo was a work of art. She had a contentment that is hard to describe. Maybe she was mad or maybe I was the crazy one, but we both seemed to be on a spiritual plain more than an earthly one.

Later walking alone I was thinking about this. Sabrina had suddenly taken flight as if prompted by the spirit with and sudden goodbye. She had embraced me like like a snake entwining her body around mine with a total sexual expression. She kissed me with passion and cried out " Oh! My God.' Then she released herself as she turned and waved once more. She was in a hurry then like she was running late for an appointment. There was no way I could keep up with her stride as she began to run.. We had reached a river crossing near Najera when she had turned and called out "I will see you again." How could I believe that, but it proved to be true. We were destined to meet again near the ruins of San Anton.

A little more sunshine and I would be an ember I was thinking. A little more blue sky and I would take flight. Something inside me spoke of the reality not the dream. Like I was striving for a hidden gem that was an impossibility to find. I was realising that letting love fantasy flow was not an answer for me. This I could see with the loves I met on the Camino. If only I had not fallen prey to my passion. If only I had remained where I was...Would I still been wondering or be in peace? All seemed grave as I sank back for a moment and vanished in a deceptive shallow like sea foam. The great dream of creativity awoke in the mist of my mind's eye. I knew then and there that I was to write many story of my journeys. They would not complete me, for they would be almost love, almost triumph but not the giving of love, just a flicker of the flame.

I recalled the advise of the sage I had met whilst in rehabilitation for depression: "Keep the flame alive, even if it be a flickering candle flame, keep it alive." Love and all that my nature endured boiled to the surface. I had fallen into the Dragon's mouth only to find it turned into a lotus flower of creative ideas. Many adventures for a life ahead lay before me. A life without boundaries to my creative expression.

CHAPTER 10.

SEREPENDITY

It was near 1200 kilometres of tramping the highways, byways, hills and dales of Northern Spain, the Wicklow Mountains of Ireland, the Aran islands and the Burren Way that I gave up the ghost. The point of it all overcame me halfway through the Burren Way. It may as well have been called the barren way, for it all seemed to me then to be unproductive. Half way up a steep hill I saw the folly of it all. Nature in Ireland from the very start of this Camino had turned against me on my weary tramping. Except for one week of fine weather and gentle breeze on the Wicklow Way it rained with ice cold winds and below average temperatures all the time. Suffering a severe influenza and a rash that just would not stop itching all over my body, it was just sheer stubborn will power that had me drive ever onward. I had beaten depression, mood swings and loneliness on that journey through the dark night of the soul. And it was the plodding onward in hope of a better life ahead that drove me. In the end God and nature had beat me. It was not just the climate but my own physical strength that failed. The journey's end found me back home in isolation and very ill for the better part of three months before I recovered.

My recall now had me back sleeping in that old caravan in the bush on a friend's property in northern New South Wales a decade or so back in time. Deep in depression after so many tragedies had befallen me, I slept a lot more than I do now. It was on one of those ghostly grey sky nights in that caravan when the moon reflected a shadow light that the child within me returned. I was shaken from my slumber with the mattress being pulled downward towards the foot of the bed. I focused my eyes to find three small boys peering pixie like holding on to the end of the mattress with a startled look in their eyes. I could not recognise them but called out: " It is all right, I am not afraid of you." I beckoned the nearest little boy to come closer and not to be afraid of me either. He slowly made his way up to the side of th bed within arms reach. He had an angelic innocent face with sparkling gentle eyes and a smile on his lips." What is your name.' I had asked : My name is Douglas " he replied. In an instant I remembered me looking up at the old man lying half depressed on the bed for I had been that little boy once and the scene back then was the reverse of the now. I turned to look at the other two boys who had not identified themselves but just as quickly all three disappeared. I turned to light the candle beside my bed to get a better prospective on what had just happened. The candle I had extinguished the night before had been erect as a lighted flame. It no longer stood upright, for in the heat of the night had melted now pointing downward like a flaccid penis. Mystified by the reality of what had transpired I fell back into a deep sleep. Upon awakening the only proof of the happening with my child self was the mattress. it had been pulled off the foot of the bed some 40 centimetres where the children had tugged at it the night before.   This perhaps was in retrospect perhaps the beginning of my creative outpouring for it was from then that I began to write poetry and short stories. I had not re-alised it until now, it was all about embracing the child within.

So it was after the long journey of my tramping that I arrived at a point of conclusion of the adventures on foot and with the pen on paper. My searching inwardly for what ailed me I had externalised into many tramps in both the southern and northern hemispheres. I had clocked up many kilometres in both Australia and New Zealand, walked the islands of Oceania, traversed the Camino from St. Jean-Pied- de-Port at the foothills of the Pyrenees in France to Santiago and on to Finis-terre; tramped mountains and plains of New Zealand and strolled the sandy beaches of the Pacific islands and slugged through rugged bush trails of Australia. I had tramped through wind, rain and sunshine in Ireland, the home of my ancestors, awakened to the torture of my own very nature. I had battled with the pain of loss of love, the torture of demons in my head and come out the other side. Equally, I had written thousands of words in stories and songs of my adventurers; poetic rhyme uncovering the unconscious thoughts and creative ex-pressions that come from the muses of my own myth. And to what avail?

Well through it all I learnt to let go to a God of my own understanding. At least from time to time this has been the case. More often than not in my own foolish wisdom I revert to the Doug thoughts of darkness and light and not that of the power that makes all things possible.Yet, I am less disturbed since gaining acceptance of the one who makes all things possible. I am not as afraid as I once was. The recognition that all things pass in time. "Trust God, all the rest is a whiff of smoke" a wise man once told me. God remains. It had been through much suf-fering and urgency that I lost my way and now he is teaching me to be patient. My heart's desire will be attained. How can I go wrong with God on my side. I have food, clothing and shelter and I am blessed to be so fortunate to live in a land of plenty when the majority of earth's people have nothing, not even food to eat nor water to drink. Yet as at now there is more than enough for all on this earth of ours if we were not so selfish as to consider the plight of our fellowman. We cannot ask the suffering ones to have faith when they have no food, lack clothing and shelter and do not have work nor the will even to survive. Prayer it is said will help but action always speaks louder than words. These thoughts drifted in and out of my head as I walked the beach, listening to the ocean roar and healing in the wind: "Not thy will but mine be done." For now all I could do was to put one foot in front of the other and keep moving forward. The demons were still hanging about in the shadows of my mind. I challenged them ..'the God of the earth and my nature is still loving and understands all things under the sun.' Then my thought drifted once more to the Jesus of my Christian upbringing. I had long since forgotten him. The one who had reportedly stated "I am the vine you are the branches," The Christian zeal was to teach us spiritual lessons to follow him in his teaching. It was all drifting back to me now. He too had suffered to free us from our defects of character. I was looking out over the bush now at a large oak tree in this autumn of my life. "…and some of us are branches, some of us leaves, some of us falling leaves, some us fallen leaves, and we all come under the power of the sun…. and the Father, the Son and the spirit are one." These words were a part of the eulogy I had uttered at my son's Peter's funeral Mass celebration.

The wind had died down and the lake I stood by was still and glistening in the afternoon sunlight. I picked up a stone and skipped it across the water. each skip left wake trails that drifted and faded to the shore. I caste another but this time it was a bigger rock that landed with a plop and the wake trails to the shore grew bigger. I watched as they slowly lapped to the shore and died. The lake was once more still.

" Still waters run deep." I heard my mind say…"winners win and losers weep." I opened my note book and wrote down a poem:

Sinking stone.

Cast a stone to water
watched the wake trails fade
life is like that fading thing
watch the ripples as they lap upon the shore.

Cast my burden like a stone
into the river of life..
watch the ripples as
they fade away upon the shore.

Feel the wind ripple the water
like loves and dreams of the past
the wake trails to the shore
it all just fades and dies.

Put down the book and the pencil
leave the old guitar aside
let go the songs of the memories
it's all wake trails to the shore.

Just fading memories of the past
they do not last for long
like wake trails to the water
like wake trails to the shore.

Wanderer on the Camino Way
footprints where there are no other
they are just markers of your steps
they fade, there is no Way.

Dreams your going further
reflections on a lake
it all just fades to nothing
like wake trails to the shore.

Like a stone cast to water
watching the wake trails fade
then looking back along the path you may
see footprints made and fading.

Pilgrim,
there is no answer , there is no way,
only wake trails to the water
All just fade away,
all just fade away.

So many thoughts and feelings, too many words and not enough silence. It was time for more contemplation and rest. Time to consider
what God had planed for me now in the afternoon of my life. I wondered with some sad feelings if I would ever wander another Camino
again, journey long distances in some strange land, face the elements
of nature anew, cross another desert with expectations of a greener
grass on the other side of the next hill or ride the ocean waves in ever
present danger of risking death in some crazy escapade or enjoy the
company of a new found friend, or find another body to hold onto and
experience   the lightening taking me away in a flash of passion to
never never land. Oh! I should not trouble myself with such wonder-
ings, for I do see myself travelling near and to far off places once more
to see another sunset in a foreign land as this old worn out man might
do. as a last hurrah before my time is at hand. No I am not the one to
take me to a deck chair on some ocean liner, rugged up against the
cold and reading the workings of some other long forgotten hero of
another dead author. Nor do I visualise at the end the pained burden
of another day to create expression into something new that fires my
imagination. It is not in my nature to do what the masses of men do. it
is no doubt true of the statement of Henry David Thoreau that "The
masses of men lead lives of quiet desperation.' but I am not one of
those for once rested and refreshed I am more inclined to his greater
quotation: "If a man does not keep pace with his companions, perhaps
it is because he hears a different drummer. Let him step to the music
which he hears, however measured or far away." I smiled to myself at

my off said expression: "I shall die climbing another mountain or mounting another woman." Well one can dream but in the end God decides.

The release after lockdown has me return to my daily rituals of relaxed contemplation, a little yoga stretching and a coffee at my local cafe to catch up on the daily newspapers or chatting with another. Still in a contemplative mood I sit and wonder as to the remainder of the day watching the passing parade of people coming and going. Their pace since Covid lockdown seems slower now despite the fact that it is morning peak hour. For me a daily plan is more measured than it was pre-Covid, when it seemed I had the need and the greater ability to multi task. Of the many things I lost or learnt during the lockdown was the need to worry about the urgent completion of many tasks at hand. Whatever is unfolding it's in God's time not mine and acceptance of what ever comes up seem to be more normal now. But I did get to thinking about my lot in life this day and what lay ahead for me. So once more I turned to my notebook and began to write another poem.

There 's an old man
at the sidewalk cafe
drinking his coffee slow
just sitting there taking it easy
no longer on the go.

Is that the old man
who made a fortune
the hero of Big Dome and CO?
didn't he see it crumble
or did he just let it go?

See the old man
at the sidewalk cafe
watching the passing parade
just sitting there taking it easy
he's no longer on the go.

Oh! he knows his time is fading
the sunset's kicking in
he can hear the bell tolling
is it ringing just for him?
He just sits there taking it in.

He's the old man
at the side walk cafe
he had lived like some Peter Pan
believed in a better way
in some Never Never land.

He knows his days are numbered
like every man that lives
knows the cards he has been dealt
are living and dying with him
so he sits there taking it in.

See the old man
at the sidewalk cafe
doing the best that he can
learning to live, love and let go
just to start all over again?

Maybe its not too late
the game of patience the go
waiting for the hand of fate
just sitting there taking it easy
with the hope of one more deal.....

before he packs it all in.

There had been so many pathways traversed and so many friendships forged on my way with fellow pilgrims. Flashbacks of days on
the road with pilgrims of all the nations of the world. I heard so many
stories, myths and legends of the past, listened to the pain of loss, the
pleasures of life and the plans for the future of so many and listened
to the lost souls who had but one thought in mind, to walk the next day
on The Way in the hope of a new beginning that may come over the
next horizon. I was thinking of Chris, my yoga teacher who had read
a quote of author Jo Coubert: "Of all the people you will know in a lifetime, you are the only one you will never leave or lose. To the question
of your life, You are the only answer. To the problems of your life, You
are the only solution." There was nothing more I could add to that
quote. For all my life expectations and experiences, for all the material possessions lost and won, for all the advice given and received, for
all the loves that came my way, for all the friendships I had known and
for those that have passed, I could but hold on to and accept the wisdom of having experienced them. It seemed a perfect reflection of my
way along this Way to Santiago and the journey of the rest of my life. I
made a note in my journal to remind myself in future melancholy moments toremember Shaw's recognition of purpose and Jo Coubert's
quote.

For a brief moment I reflected on those ghostly Avatars that had visited me on my journeys. In particular that of Christ who taught that my
suffering and handing over to the will to God would give me spiritual
awareness and lead me to his purpose for me. I had often prayed in
my youth for God to enlighten me to my purpose in life and now it was
unfolding in the form of creative pursuits. I visualised another guided

meditation by Fr. John Maine who devoted his priestly life to teach an ancient meditative practice on devotion to Christ and his guidance. It seemed that not only did I have visitations from God's Avatars of devotion to their own link to the heavenly Father, but in fact was being led by their example whilst on this earthly plain. It was like they were opening a door for me into the light of my own soul purpose. For a brief moment I saw the great old Major General, Count Cherep-Spiridovick of Russia. I heard him again voice his influence from his writings whilst on this earthly plain in the early years of the 20th century. He had warned from his intimate knowledge the of the rise of Bolshevism, the coming of world wars and the dangers of a one world government that would transpire in the future. In his 1913 published prophetic book: " Towards Disaster, Danger and Remedies.'" all his predictions had come to pass in the 20th century and his wisdom of the traps of the hand in the dark for the future of the material world were now in play as well as the virus predictions that would come in plague portions, the lockdowns that would happen worldwide of which we are now enduring. He spoke with some forceful advice to me to keep up my writing, to promote his vision and that of Godly purpose- and I promised him I would attempt to do before he fade from my mind and view. It was not just me who recognised his ability, the International press of the second half of the 20th century recognised him as a" Prophetic genius." . Such guidance from the Avatars of my Camino's on the Santiago Way, the Wicklow Way, the Aran islands, the Burren Way and my many tramps in Australia and New Zealand have influenced and guided me on my way.

In these final words of the snippets of my travels I see fading images of those great authors I met at the " Wicklow Heather" on the Wicklow Way, and the ghostly image of the priest old Wicklow himself the toothless one. Then the image of Tom the Irishman on our walk along broad-walk of Galway Bay. I feel sure he was an incarnation of St. Patrick himself, the Saint of the Isle, for he had so many stories to tell of the goodly saint's travel. I feel sure if the weather had not turned fowl and driven us to separate shelters in Galway, Tom would still be still standing talking of the feat and faith of the infamous Patrick.

My return to my home to memories both real and imagined gave me some solace of the value of stepping out there into the great unknown. However, it is only memory. For of the now there is today and a new season in the making for another new beginning.

To every thing (turn, turn, turn.)
there is a season (turn, turn, turn.)
and a time to every purpose, under heaven.

A time to be born, a time to die
a time to plant, a time to reap
a time to kill, a time to heal
a time to laugh, a time to weep

To everything (turn, turn, turn.)
there is a season (turn, turn, turn.)
and a time to every purpose under heaven

A time to build up, a time to break down
a time to dance, a time to mourn
A time to cast away stones, a time to gather stones together

To everything (turn, turn, turn.)
there is a season (turn, turn, turn.)
and a time to every purpose under heaven

A time to love, a time to hate
a time of war, a time of peace
a time you may embrace, a time to refrain from embracing

to everything (turn, turn, turn.)
there is a season (turn, turn, turn.)
and a time to every purpose under heaven.

A time to gain, a time to lose
a time to rend, a time to sew
a time of love, a time of hate
a time to return to embracing .

A time to be born, a time to die
a time to plant, a time to reap
a time to kill, a time to heal
a time to laugh, a time to reap.

To everything turn! turn! turn!
there is a season
 and a time to every purpose under heaven.

CHAPTER 11.

CONCLUSIONS

Much of the words between the covers of this book are based on truth and some are based on the fiction of a fertile imagination. It is for the reader to determine what is real and what is fantasy and I as the writer makes no apology for leaving you to do that. I also make no apology for limiting subject matter as a kind of challenge to the reader to re-search proof of fact. Before I began to write this book I had the end in mind to fit it all into 100 pages. Therefore , I could only fit concise de-tails of information to support my story within these limits. I leave to you the reader to do further research that may be to your liking if you consider it necessary for your need on deeper meaning of truth, poetic expression or in sorting the fact from fiction, the proof of truth and myth of lies. The history books in my seven decades plus on this earthly plain have been altered many times to suit those in power to manipulate all with false education to suit their will and purpose. What I studied during my years of education to understand and to get ahead in this world has, to a great degree, been erased from the courses of learning. A modern day methodology of dumbing down the education system for the masses continues to be pliable to the hands of the so called hands in the dark.

The characters I have used here to support my story and what I have come to understand for the benefit of all concerned are as real as the history books of religion and ethics would have us believe. As real as any of the previous stories I have written from my imagination and researched on my own road less travelled. It has been necessary for me to write, to understand the world we live in and the paths taken to get where I am now. To open up in my findings to a guiding path from the present cave of the mind to the outer world of freedom and best survival for me and those in whom I trust and care for. I have done much research to support the account of   the workings of my mind and the link I have with the spirits of the past, the muses that have in-fluenced me in all the books I have written to this date. I trust this will continue to be so in the interest of you the reader, your journey of life's purpose and discoveries. There will be many new faces we shall both encounter on the way; new characters, new places and new creative ideas that may spring forth for you and for me as a consequence. Characters here I tell in this little book are sometimes real and some imaginary tales manifested to truth,. They are but a snippet of the story of my own journey of life coloured by my own imagination, sup-ported by Pilgrims I met along the way and the guiding lights from the other side in my conclusions of belief and disbelief I have experienced as a result.

My journey of life and the recent lockdown of Covid-19 has had me come to realise that I am not an island unto myself but a part of the whole community of life. One of the marvellous things about community is that it enables us to welcome and help people in a way we couldn't as individuals. When we pool our strength and share the work and responsibility, we can welcome many people, even those in deep distress, and perhaps help them find self-confidence and inner healing. A community is only being created when its members accept that they are not going to achieve great things, that they are not going to be heroes, but simply live each day with new hope, like children, in wonderment as the sun rises and in thanksgiving as it sets. Community is only being created when people recognise that the greatness of man is to accept his insignificance, his human condition and his earth, and to thank God for having put in a finite body the seeds of eternity, which are visible in small and daily gestures of love and forgiveness. The beauty of man is in this fidelity to the wonder of each day. I trust that my little written works add some value to that course. So it is for now that I turn to listening for the still small voices that lay within to guide me to and for what ever it is that I am to do and to be in this the afternoon of my life.

Listening

Stick man plays a drum solo
Bass man picks up the beat,
Guitarist plays some melody
adds some slide to make it zing.

Oh! The singer he's off key
just not with the tune
his minds on some Camino,

Cause,
he's not listening,
no, he's not listening,

Mary's a walking companion,
she's on the road from love,
wants him to give her a baby,
he's not in the mood for love.

Lot's wife her mind wanders,
looking for what might have been
he tells her not to look back

but she's not listening, no she's not listening.

The singer picks up a walking beat,
he's singing s different tune
spoke to Lot along The Way
his wife was a pillar of salt.

Oh! the singer is a stick man
walking to his down beat
hears the sound of the drummer
in the magic of his feet.

Now the singer is a wanderer
no drums, no bass , no guitar
the only sound of rhythm
the movement of his feet.

The singer, the lover, the poet,
the music of dancing feet,
intone with a love triangle
in the tapping of his feet.

Do you hear the sound of
the drummer,
the rhythm and the beat,
pick the vibes of the Bass and guitar,
the movement of your feet.

Is it in the guitar melody
maybe its in the slide
stop for a while along the way
listen fro a while

Now the singer is a wanderer
no drum, no bass , no guitar
He's hearing the sound
of the music now
ing the tapping of his feet,

Cause,
he is listening,
yes, he is listening.

"God
Grand me the serenity,
to accept the things I cannot change,
courage to change the things I can,
and the wisdom to know the difference."

About the Author.

Doug McPhillips, poet, singer, songwriter, author, commenced his journey of discovery over a decade ago after life changing experiences.

The many tracks he has traversed throughout the Northern Hemisphere and down under in New Zealand and Australia has resulted in the facts and fictions of this novel.

Doug has recorded and sings songs interrelated to his work with majestic melody in a true Australian style.

Doug has written five novels, two book of poems, a travel guide and two albums of his songs of which all are inspired by his adventurers.

www.caminoway.com.au

"A journey of the Spirit."

Doug is an adventurer who divides his time between creative pursuits, love for family and of friends, and those who may benefit most from his efforts and experience.

Worldwide Publishers.
Ingram Sparke
1 La Verge TN37086
Nashville Tennessee.

Printed in Australia
Lightning Source Australia
76 Discovery Road South
Scoresby, Victoria 3179

102

Galway Bay.

If you ever go across the sea to Ireland,
then maybe at the closing of your day,
you can sit and watch the moon rise over Claddaugh
and see the sun go down on Galway Bay.

Just to hear again the ripple of the trout stream,
the women in the meadows making hay,
or to sit beside the turf fire in a cabin,
and watch the barefoot godsons as they play.

Ooh

For the breezes blowing o'er the sea's from Ireland,
are perfumed by the heather as they blow,
and the women in the upland digging praties,
speak a language that the strangers do not know.

Yet the strangers came and tried to teach us their ways,
they scorned us just for being what we are,
but they might as well go chasing after moonbeams ,
or light a penny candle from a star.

And if there's going to be a life here after,
and somehow I am sure there's going to be,
I will ask my God to let me make my heaven,
in that dear land across the Irish sea.

I will ask my God to let me make my heaven,
in that dear land across the Irish sea.

15/11/21.

.